Twelve Weeks To Midnight Blue

KidVenture Vol. I

by Steve Searfoss

ISBN 9781672411417

Library of Congress Control Number: 2019920360

Colossians 3:23

www.kidventurebook.com

Table of Contents

for Sebastian

who inspires me
by always putting people first
and wanting to do things the right way.

Chapter 1

Midnight Blue

If anyone tells you that kids can't start a business, don't listen to them. They can. I should know, because I did. People sometimes ask me how KidVenture started and how it got its name. Well, I'll tell you. It all started the summer before sixth grade. All I remember about that summer is that it was hot, so hot I thought I would melt. That and my sister Addison kept annoying me. You could say I was boiling and steaming that summer.

My dad told me he would pay me ten bucks to clean the pool. It was a pretty good deal. I'd take a net and scoop out all the leaves and dead bugs that had landed in the water. It took me about two hours to clean the pool so I figure I was making about five dollars an hour. Not bad for a ten-year-old kid.

I thought it was going to be a one-time gig, but the following week my dad asked me if I wanted to clean the pool again.

"But I already did," I said. He told me to go take a look. I couldn't believe it. The pool was full of leaves and dead bugs again. I had spent all the money I made from cleaning the pool the week before on a slingshot, two comic books and an ice cream cone. I needed the cash so I said yes.

Next thing you know, I'm cleaning the pool every week and making an easy ten bucks each time. After a couple weeks, I realized I could save my money and buy that bicycle I had seen one time at that big sporting goods store on Wilson Street. The bike was super cool. When I looked at the sticker, it said the color was midnight blue. I didn't know what that meant, except that it sounded dangerous and I liked that. I asked my dad if we could get it and he said, *we'll see,* which is the grown-up way of saying *No, but I want to let you down easy.*

The bike, the dangerous one, cost $225. Which is way more money than a ten-year-old could ever hope to get. That is, unless said impoverished ten-year-old had a job, which I now apparently had.

"It's going to take forever to save up for that bike," I said, after I had just finished cleaning the pool for the second time, and my dad handed me a crisp ten dollar bill.
"No, not forever," my dad retorted. "You'll save up $225 in no time."
"Not when I'm only making ten bucks a week." I started to feel sorry for myself and walked away.
Then I turned around. "Dad, how long will it take if I save all my pool cleaning money?"
"You figure it out," my dad said, and handed me a paper and pencil.
"But I hate math!" I protested.
"Well then you're right. It *will* take forever," my dad said and returned to reading his newspaper.
"Oh all right," I sighed. "Hand me the pencil."

I started scribbling some numbers.

"Twenty…Twenty-two…Twenty-three! No, wait. Twenty-two and a half weeks!" I shouted excitedly.
"How many months is that?" my dad asked.
"Ugh. More math? Seriously?"
"Seriously."

My dad has a way with words. I began scribbling numbers again.
"Let's see, four weeks in a month, approximately, so that works out to…" I mumbled.

Bike $225
Pool Money $10 per week
$225 / $10 = 22.5 weeks

4 weeks per month (approx.)
22.5 / 4 = 5.625 months

4.25 weeks per month (exact)
22.5 / 4.25 = 5.29 months

"Five-point-six-two-five months." I said triumphantly.
"That's right," my dad smiled. "So about five and a half months."
"Wait…" I said dejectedly. "Oh no!"
"What?"
"That's five and a half months, if I don't buy any more ice cream."
"True."
"Better call it six months."
"Six months is not a long time," my dad insisted.
"It is!" I scowled. "At this rate I might was well just wait till Christmas."

A couple more weeks went by, and even though I dreamed of mint chocolate chip ice cream almost every night, I had managed to save all of my pool money. I had $30 tucked away in my bike fund when I suddenly had an idea.

I went straight to my dad and declared, "Dad! Dad! I have an idea."
He put his newspaper down slowly and raised an eyebrow.
"Yes?"
I could barely contain myself. "How about you pay me $20 for cleaning the pool!"
"$20?"

"Yes! Yes! Twenty buckaroos. I can't believe I didn't think of this sooner. Twenty dollars for cleaning the pool instead of ten."

"Hm....I like it."

"You do?" I have to admit, even as excited as I was, I wasn't really expecting the conversation to go so well.

"You're negotiating," my dad said. "I like that."

"Great!" I exclaimed. "Wait, what's negotiating?"

"It's what you're doing now," my dad said. "Asking for more."

"Great! Awesome. So, is that a *yes*?"

"No."

"But why not? I'm negotiating, just like you said."

"Yes," my dad said. And then he smiled. I recognized that same smile. It was the smile he had when he told me when I was three years old that Santa had made a wrong turn somewhere east of Winnipeg on his way to our house and there would be no Christmas presents that year.

"You're forgetting that *I'm* negotiating too."

My mom had her own smile. It was the smile that immediately told my dad to stop making the children cry on Christmas Eve.

"And I want to know," my Dad continued, still smiling, "why would I pay more for the exact same pool cleaning service you're already providing for the handsome sum of $10."

I had to admit he had a point. Where was Mom? I could really use her help right now.

"You raise an interesting question," I said, trying to sound as serious as I could. "I'll have to think about that and get back to you."

I couldn't sleep that night. I was thinking about what I could do that would be different than just the same pool cleaning service I offered. What could I offer my dad that would be of more value, so I could charge more?

What do *you* think?

How could you charge more for the same service?

What would you do differently?

Chapter 2

Mr. Danger

"I got it!" I leaped out of bed and ran down the hall and started knocking on my dad's door.

No answer. I knocked harder.

"What is it?" I heard a very grumpy voice say.

"I'm ready to negotiate."

"No negotiations until morning." The voice got grumpier. "Now go back to bed!"

When it was finally morning I was waiting at the breakfast table ready to pounce. My dad came in and while he was pouring some coffee I said, "Ok, here is my proposal." I tried to sound as official as I could.

"Hmpf…Negotiating before I've had my first cup of coffee?" My dad said, half sleepy and half amused. "That's dangerous."

"My middle name is danger," I said confidently.

"Actually, it's Robert."

"Yes well…" I stammered. "Don't mess up my flow here…I'm about to get on a roll."

"Proceed then, Mr. Danger." My dad took a sip of his coffee.

"Well, I thought about what you said, and I have to admit you have a point. You've been paying me $10 to clean the pool. But you've also had to remind me several times to clean the pool, so basically you've been paying me $10 to physically remove the dead leaves and bugs, and other debris from the pool, and let's say for the sake of argument that's worth ten dollars."

"Yes, let's say that," my dad, in fact, said.

Just then my sister Addison walked in and poured herself some orange juice.

I cleared my throat dramatically. "What I propose is a pool cleaning service, where you don't have to worry about your pool being clean, you don't have to ever remind me. Instead, I guarantee that the pool will be cleaned every week by noon on Friday, so it's ready for a weekend of swimming action."

"That sounds interesting." My dad raised an eyebrow. "Go on."

"What I'm offering, then, is not just a clean pool, but peace of mind. You don't have to worry again whether the pool will be clean, and you don't have to remind me to do it."

"I like it," my dad said.

"And you can have this peace of mind for the small sum of ten dollars a week." I smiled broadly, proud of myself. I was particularly proud of the *for the small sum* bit. I heard that on the radio once and liked it. "So $20 total."

My dad whistled his surprise. "So you're doubling the price?" he challenged.

"Small price to pay for peace of mind," I countered.

"Fifteen," my dad said.

I mumbled for a bit, unsure of what to say. I finally recovered enough to blurt out, "But the price is 20!"

I stared at my dad intently, narrowing my eyes and furrowing my forehead, much the way I imagine a cheetah does when it spots a gazelle that looks like dinner on the African savanna. Did I mention my middle name is Robert? That's French for dangerous.

My dad stared back. He didn't scowl like a cheetah. He simply stared at me, to see if I would flinch.

I gulped.

The stare-down continued. Who knew a gazelle could be that fierce?

"The price is $20," I said evenly.

"I'll do it for $10!" my sister suddenly interjected.

"What?!" My dad and I said at the same time and turned towards her.

"Addison!" I shouted. "You stay out of this."

"I'll do it for $10," she insisted. "I'll clean the pool and also that whole peace of mind thingamajig."

7

"Fine! $15 and not a penny more!" I stretched out my hand and walked towards my father. "But you must decide now."

He looked at me and smiled. "You have a deal."

"We have a deal." I shook his hand very dramatically so he wouldn't change his mind.

"No fair!" Addie cried out. "Why does he get to do it? I offered to do it for less."

"Well, I already know he can do the job, and I rather stick with one vendor right now."

"What's a vendor?" Addie asked.

"A vendor is someone who sells you a product, or in this case a service," Dad explained.

"In other words, I am a vendor and you're not." I smirked.

"But I want to be a vendor!"

"You didn't even know what a vendor was five minutes ago and now you want to be one," I said.

"Daddy! No fair, why does he get to be a vendor and I don't?"

"We'll think of something for you Addie, don't worry." My dad poured himself a second cup of coffee.

"Hey Dad, if you know I can do the job and you trust me as a vendor already, why don't you pay $20?"

"It's called leverage, Son."

"What does that mean?"

"It means there are two possible vendors bidding for the same job. Two vendors, only one client. Two of you, and only one of me. Who has the power to say no?"

I swallowed slowly and thought about it. "Um...uh...I suppose you do."

"And why's that?"

"Because if you say no to me, then you have Addie who can clean the pool. But if I say no to you, I don't have anyone else and I'm out of a job."

"Smart kid. Leverage is about who has more options."

"Thanks a lot Addie! Thanks to you I just lost five dollars a week."

"That's a small price to pay to learn about leverage," my dad said.

"You'll thank your sister one day."
"I doubt it."

"I agree! You *should* be thanking me now," Addie said, gulping down the last of her orange juice.
"No way."
"So… How long before you can buy your bike?" my dad changed the subject.
"That'll be another five or six months."
"Will it?"
"Well *yeah*," I said annoyed. I was still thinking about how my sister had ruined my deal.
"But you're making 50% more a week now," my dad said
"So?"
"So if you're earning more per week, doesn't that get you to your goal faster?"
I rubbed my chin. "Oh yeah…"
My dad pushed paper and pencil across the table. "Math is your friend," he said.
"With friends like this, who needs enemies!"
My dad looked at me without saying a word. I had already lost one stare-down that morning, so I took the paper and pencil and started working.
Let's see, I mumbled to myself. *Two hundred twenty five divided by 15 equals 15. And divided by four equals three point seventy five.*
I put the pencil down. "Fifteen weeks."
"How many months is that?" my dad asked.
"I knew you would ask that." I smiled. "Three and three quarters. Almost four."
"That's a lot better than 5 1/2 months," my dad smiled back.
"It sure is."
"In fact, it will only take 2/3 as long to buy your bike at this new $15 rate."
"Really?"
"Do the math."
"Argh. Ok." I picked up the pencil again. "You're right, it'll take

66.6% of the time it would have taken at $10 per week."
"Correct."
"Plus I already have $30 saved up." I had been cleaning Dad's pool for four weeks by then. I wished I had saved my money after that first week, instead of spending it on ice cream and comic books. I was one third into the summer and had earned thirty dollars.
"Great."
"Maybe I can have Midnight Blue by the time school starts."
"Keep working hard and saving Son, and I'm sure you will."
I raised my hand as if taking an oath. "But I still don't like math!"

Bike $225
Pool Money $15 per week
$225 / $15 = 15 weeks

4 weeks per month (approx.)
15 / 4 = 3.75 months

$15 per week new rate
$10 per week old rate
15/10 = 1.5
1.5 - 1 = 0.5
0.5 * 100 = 50% increase

@ $10 per week = 22.5 weeks to buy bike
@ $15 per week = 15 weeks to buy bike
22.5 - 15 = 7.5 weeks less time
15 / 22.5 = 66.6% = 2/3 time to bike

"Good morning!" My mom walked into the kitchen carrying my baby brother, my little sister in tow. "How are my entrepreneurs doing?"

"Doing good, I suppose. Dad agreed to pay $15 for cleaning the pool so I get my bike a lot faster now.

"That's wonderful honey. Are you ready for some breakfast?"

"Sorry Mom, I've got to go."

"Where are you going?"

"I'm on a mission."

"Oh? A mission for what?"

"I've got to go find some leverage." I grabbed an apple and put it in my pocket and ran out the door. "Bye Mom!"

"Be careful!" she called after me. She always says that.

As soon as I was at the front door I started thinking. How could I get more leverage?

What do *you* think?

How could you get more leverage?

What could you do to generate more options?

Chapter 3

Sir Larry

I headed over to Cherry Hills, which had a lot of big houses, the kind I figured would have a pool in the back yard. It was about a ten or fifteen minute walk from my house. It was hot. Did I mention it was really hot that summer? I thought about stopping at the convenience store on the corner of Oak & Maple St. to buy an ice cream sandwich, but then I remembered my goal. Buying ice cream would just add more time before I could buy Midnight Blue. But it sure was hot.

As I walked over, I practiced what I would say to get a new customer. *May I interest you in our pool cleaning service? Do you need more than just a clean pool? Do you need reliability, promptness and peace of mind? How would you like to have a clean pool every week? There are clean pools, and then there are clean pools. Clean! Clean! Clean! And for the low, low price of $20.*

When I got to the first house on the street I paused for a moment, took a deep breath, and knocked on the door. No answer. This time I knocked more forcefully. Still no answer.

Ok, no problem. I moved on to the next house and knocked. No response. I knocked again. Still nothing. I knocked louder. Oh well, on to the next one. I knocked on the next door. Three times. No answer. Ok, so maybe this was going to be harder than I thought.

Five more doors and I finally got a response. A nice old lady opened the door and before I could get two words in she disappeared into her foyer and returned a couple minutes later and handed me some candy.

"You seem nice," she said. "Have some candy."

"I can clean your pool."

"Oh you don't need to do that," she smiled. "I'm happy to give it to you. I keep a bowl of candy in my kitchen for guests. It's leftover from Halloween. You're welcome to have some."

"I mean for $20."

"You want me to give you $20?"

"Yes."

She was horrified.

Oops. "No, no," I said. "I don't want $20. I mean, I do want $20." I stammered. "But I don't mean for you to just give me $20. I mean I will clean your pool for $20."

She still looked confused.

"I'm grateful for the candy, Ma'am."

"Oh, why didn't you say so. I don't have a pool." She seemed relieved.

"Oh." I smiled awkwardly. "Well, I'll be going now. Thank you for the candy."

I sat on the curb and as I bit into one of the candy bars she gave me. I had to admit I wasn't feeling great. They always made it look so easy in the movies. I thought for sure I'd have a new client by now. After all, I was a *vendor* now, not just a kid. I was offering a clean pool and peace of mind at a good price.

After a few minutes of feeling sorry for myself I got back up and knocked on the next door. And the door after that. And the door after that one. And four more doors after that. Finally, someone answered. A pimply teenager wearing a backwards baseball cap.

I started telling him about my pool cleaning services when he said, "hold on a second", pulled out his phone and start taking notes. *This is good*, I thought. He's really interested. I explained it's a weekly service, he could pick the day and time and I would be there at that time to clean his pool.

"So it's not just a clean pool, it's peace of mind for the low, low price of $20." The last part I sang like a jingle. Just like I'd heard on the radio.

"That's really good," he said.

"Awesome. So you'll do it?"

"Oh no," he said quickly. "I need some money this summer and this sounds like a good way to make some extra money."

"Hey!" I shouted. "No fair! It's my idea."

"Cleaning pools is your idea?" he asked sarcastically.

"Yes!"

"No it's not. Anyone can clean pools."

"Not like this, not like I can."

"Whatever dude." He waved his hand dismissively.

"Yeah dude, whatever." It was all I could think of saying and stormed off.

Well that didn't go down as I'd planned. I didn't have a single new customer and I'd possibly created a competitor. I was losing leverage, not gaining it.

I was ready to give up. Who cares about Midnight Blue, I thought. I could just wait till Christmas and hope to get it then. I bit into the last piece of candy the nice old lady gave me. I was starting to appreciate just how nice she had been. It felt good to chew something sweet as I contemplated my future.

I decided to press on and keep trying. Not because of Midnight Blue, but because of my dad. I didn't want to go back and admit defeat. Not after vowing I'd find more leverage. I didn't want him to see me give up.

I knocked on twenty more doors after that. Most people weren't home. One woman told me she already had a pool cleaning service and wasn't interested. Another told me she would think about it, and another told me she didn't have a pool, but if she did, she would definitely want me to clean it.

I finally struck gold on my final attempt of the day. It was the last house on the street, and I had already decided I was going home after that. I knocked on the door and a very large man wearing sunglasses opened the door.

"I can clean your pool for $20." I was too tired to say everything I'd been practicing to say. I was even too tired to put on my radio voice, the one that says in a singsong, *and for the low, low price of $20.*

He looked at me, almost confused.

"Look, I'm just a kid trying to make a little extra money this summer," I blurted out.
He smiled. "I like that. You remind me of my son."
Uh-oh. Not another competitor. "Does your son clean pools too?"
"Not anymore. He's away in college now, but he used to mow lawns."
"Oh, that's a good idea."
"How much?"
"Twenty dollars. And I promise I'll do a good job."
"Come back on Tuesday at 11 and if you do a good job I'll hire you every week."
"Really?!" After knocking on who knows how many doors, I couldn't believe it.
"Yeah sure, let's try it. I like that you're working hard to earn a little extra money."
"Deal!" I practically squealed as I stretched out my hand to shake his.

Maybe that pimply teenager had the right idea after all. Here I had my first customer who wasn't my dad, and I didn't even have to use my radio voice or any fancy sales pitches. Maybe being a kid willing to work hard was enough.

"Thank you sir! I will be here on Tuesday at 11."

"Call me Larry."

"Yes sir. I mean Larry. Sorry sir. Larry! Very nice to meet you Sir Larry!"

He chuckled.

"Yes sir. Yes Larry!" I was so excited and nervous I was shaking his hand like a madman. "I'm Chance. Chance Sterling. Very nice to meet you Larry. I'll be here on Tuesday. I can't wait. I'll do a really good job. I promise."

I started to walk back home ecstatic. I couldn't wait to tell my dad I got a new client. And he was willing to pay $20! That's $5 more than my dad paid. I had leverage now.

Then I looked at my watch. I had been out knocking on doors for four hours. That's a long time. It only takes two hours to clean a pool. Twenty dollars divided by two is $10 an hour. Not bad for a ten-year-old. Not bad at all. But if I add the four hours it took me to find Sir Larry, that's six hours total. That works out to $3.33 per hour. That's not so good. That's bad, actually. So if Larry hires me only once and doesn't ask me to come back, that's not such a great deal. Now if Larry has me come back a second time, then I've made $40 between the two times. And it took me 8 hours: 4 hours cleaning the pool, plus four hours looking for a new customer and finding Larry. That works out to five dollars an hour. Not great, but getting better.

Whenever I cleaned my dad's pool I would get $15 –that was our new deal–, which works out to $7.50 an hour. I kept running numbers in my head as I walked home. But don't tell my dad I was doing math. If I cleaned Larry's pool three times, that would be $60 for 10 hours of work. That's $6 an hour. Getting better. If I cleaned Larry's pool four times that's $80 for 12 hours of work. That's $6.66

per hour. Definitely better, but not yet as good as the $7.50 I would be making with my dad.

Now if I could clean Larry's pool five weeks in a row, that would be $100 for 14 hours of work. That's $7.14 an hour. It's only after six times cleaning Larry's pool, that I would make $7.50 per hour.

$15 to clean Dad's pool
2 hours to clean pool
$15 / 2 = $7.50 per hour

$20 to clean Larry's pool
2 hours to clean pool
4 hours to find Larry
2 + 4 = 6 hours
$20 / 6 = $3.33 per hour

Clean Larry's pool twice
$20 x2 = $40
(2x2) hrs cleaning + 4hrs finding Larry = 8 hours
$40 / 8 = $5 per hour

Clean Larry's pool 6 times
(6x2) hrs cleaning + 4hrs finding Larry = 16 hours
$120 / 16 = $7.50 per hour

Wow, that's a lot of work. I better do a really good job next Tuesday, I thought. *And hope Larry keeps me on for the summer.* On the plus side, if I could clean Larry's pool eight times that would be $8 an hour!

That made me think. There had to be a better way to find new clients than knocking on doors in the hot sun. If I could find a way to find a new client in less than four hours, I could make more money. But how could I do that?

What do *you* think?

Is there an easier way to find clients?

What else could you try?

Chapter 4

Now It's Official

I was in the backyard practicing soccer kicks, relaxing after a tough morning knocking on doors looking for new customers. It felt good to kick the ball hard and see it swoosh into the back of the net. It was a small beat-up goal. I think I got it for my sixth birthday. That was a really long time ago. It seemed huge at the time, but as I've gotten older it felt smaller and smaller. Which was perfect because I could practice my accuracy, kicking from longer distances and strange angles to see if I could get the ball into the small net.

I was pretty good. I'd say I got the ball in the net about 60% or 70% of the time. Which made me wonder about what I was doing trying to get customers. Even though Larry had agreed to hire me to clean his pool, it had still been a frustrating experience. I had easily knocked on fifty or more doors. I thought about it, and figured out that works out to 2%. Two percent! So for every hundred kicks I took, only two we're going to go into the net. Who wants to play that game? Not me.

Plus, how did I know Larry answering the door and saying yes wasn't just pure dumb luck? I didn't. Since there was only one person who signed up for my pool cleaning service, I couldn't assume there would be a new customer every time. The sample size was way too small. Now if three or four had said yes, then maybe I could assume roughly those same odds every time. But one yes could just be random. I could kick a hundred soccer balls an afternoon and make 60 goals one day and 70 the next. I could reliably score somewhere in that range. If I did it four more times I would make 64, 72, 61, and 67 goals. I know, because I actually spent the next week writing down the number of goals I made each

time I'd practice in the backyard. So it's safe to assume a 66% average success rate, give or take.

But after only one outing looking for customers and knocking on doors for hours, could I even assume a 2% success rate? No. If I did it again the next day and no one answered, I'd be looking at best at a 1% rate and, at worst, confirmation that Larry was an outlier, a random result that couldn't be trusted to repeat.

The thought of going out there again made me anxious. I tried to imagine spending four hours knocking on doors again and coming back empty. There had to be a better way to find new customers.

As I thought about it, I realized just how inefficient it was to go around knocking on doors. For one thing, most people weren't home when I went around knocking in the morning. Maybe they were already out at work. So that was a problem. I wanted to tell them about my pool cleaning service at a time that they weren't available, or ready to listen. And on top of that, when someone did answer the door, I had no idea whether they even had a pool or not. That was my second problem. I was wasting a lot of time knocking on the doors of empty houses, trying to figure out if the person I was talking to even had a pool.

I had to find a way to solve those two problems. I had to think of a way to only talk to people who were ready to listen, and who had a pool. People who might be interested in the service I offered. Knocking on doors of empty houses or talking to people without a pool was wasting my time. And, as my dad would say, time is money.

Take 100 shots on goal
Make 65 goals
65 / 100 = 65% success rate

Take 100 shots on goal 4 times
Make 64, 72, 61, 67 goals
(64 + 72 + 61 + 67) / 4 = 66% average success rate

Knock on 50 doors
Get 1 new client
1 / 50 = 2% success rate

Knock on 50 doors again
Get 0 new clients
0 / 50 = 0% success rate

1 / 100 = 1% average success rate

The question was, how? My brain hurt from thinking so much, so I went back to kicking the ball. I moved it back further and further from the net to challenge myself. It felt good to score goals. Lots of goals.

That evening I got to the dinner table early, hoping to catch my dad alone so I could talk to him without Addie hearing. When he arrived, I was grinning so wide and so hard I thought my jaw would fall off.

"What are you so happy about?" my dad asked.
"Leverage. That's what." Then I saw Addie walk into the room and my grin turned into a frown. "Can I speak to you privately?" I said under my breath.
"No," my dad said. "We don't have secrets in this family."
"But this is important," I insisted. "I don't want my sister to hear it."
"All the more reason to just say whatever you're going to say." Dad held firm.
Addie beamed.
"Ok." I took a deep breath. "I have a new client."
"Oh really?"
"Really. And they're willing to pay $20 to have their pool cleaned."
"That's great!" My dad gave me a high five. I wasn't expecting that. "Congratulations Son."
"Uh…thanks Dad."

My dad turned his attention to the stack of mail on the table. My mom peeked in to announce we were having leftovers and it would just be a few more minutes to warm them up. I could hear my baby brother in the other room crying while my little sister was singing to him to distract him.
"Uh, Dad?"
"Yes, Chance?" He didn't even look up.
"So…Dad." I leaned forward to get his attention. "I decided my new, and official, cleaning rate is twenty dollars."
"That's great Son."

"Twenty buckaroos."

"Uh-huh." My dad mumbled.

"Did I mention it was official?"

"I believe you did."

"So…then…" I paused to clear my throat dramatically. "I want $20 for cleaning the pool." I shot my sister a look that basically said, *don't you dare say anything*. But strange enough, she actually seemed uninterested.

"Oh," my dad said, surprised. I couldn't tell if he was actually surprised, or just pretending to be surprised.

"Well, I did say it was official."

"I didn't know if official meant it applied to family."

"Yes, that's exactly what it means," I said hurriedly.

"But we're family. Don't we get a special rate?"

"I have leverage now, Dad, just like you taught me."

My dad furrowed his brow. "Ok, I accept your terms, but on one condition."

"What's that?"

"Well if we're going to pay the official rate just like any other client, then I will treat you just like any other vendor."

I flashed a quick, nervous look at my mom. "Wait, what does that mean?…I don't get Christmas presents anymore?"

"No, no, no," my dad chuckled. "Of course you still do. You're still my son. Except when you clean our pool, you are now…what's that word?…" My dad smiled. "Oh yes, *officially* a vendor." When he said the word officially he drew it out, as if it had ten f's in it. Offffffffficially.

I gulped.

"Ok, I said, not sure what I was agreeing to. "You have a deal." I shook his hand. And then I spent the rest of dinner quiet, wondering what it meant to officially be a vendor to my dad. Just like any other vendor. What did he mean by that?

What do *you* think?

What does it mean to be treated like any other vendor?

Was it a good idea to ask for more?

Chapter 5

Nervous Spaghetti

There was a clump of leaves that had clustered together in the far corner of the pool into the shape of a half moon. Or at least, if you squinted real hard and used your imagination, it was a half moon. Mostly it just looked like soggy leaves, but I liked to imagine I saw shapes and patterns and not just random debris floating in the pool. It made the time go faster. *Look, there's a starfish. Sort of. And over there is an arrow. Kind of. And a stop sign.*

I scooped up the moon, the starfish, the arrow, stop sign and a bunch of stragglers with a big net and dumped them into a bucket. Then I switched to a smaller net to scoop up the dead insects bobbing along the surface. This one I could use with just one hand, not like the big net, where I had to use both arms to lift and maneuver it.

I liked to pretend the bugs were still alive and swimming, trying to get away. I'd reach down with the net and they would say, *No please, no, don't scoop me up.* I reached over for a pair of bees. *Swim faster! I can't, I'm swimming as fast as I can.* Too late. With a quick flick of the wrist they were mine. I saw another glinting in the water. *Don't think you can get away, Mr. Dragonfly. I see you.* Then I switched to a silly voice in my head. *Oh no! I was hoping you didn't see me.* I lunged and with one quick scoop lifted it out of the water and into the bucket.

Once I was done scooping up leaves and insects, I pulled all the drains and cleared out all of the gunk in them with my hands. The bucket was more than two-thirds full by the time I was done. I was getting better at this. I checked my watch: one hour and forty-five minutes. Not bad. When summer first started it would take me more than two hours, sometimes two-and-a-half, if I took breaks. But I didn't take breaks anymore. My goal was to see if I could clean the pool in an hour and a half. Maybe by the end of summer.

When I was done, I emptied the bucket of debris into our large trashcan and I put up the nets. I headed to the kitchen for some of my mom's iced tea. Addie was at the table drawing. She was always doing art. Ponies and puppies, bears and bunnies, that sort of thing. Lots of pinks and purples, sparkles and glitter. Girly stuff. Rainbows and sunsets. *Boring* stuff, if you ask me.

I reached into the fridge, poured myself a glass and took a big gulp. Ah, that felt good. I downed the full glass and then poured myself another one. As I sipped it I flipped through the newspaper my dad had left on the counter. Nothing caught my eye. Then I glanced over at what Addie was drawing. *I bet she's drawing a unicorn or something just as silly—*

"Wait a minute! Addie! What are you drawing?" I said, shocked. She quickly scooped up her papers and stuffed them into her sketchbook and closed the cover. Mighty suspicious.
"Nothing." She grinned.
"That didn't look like nothing."
"Just drawing."
"What were you doing?"
"Why do you care?" she said defensively.
"I want to know."
"It's none of your business."
"Oh, it *is* my business." I glared at her. "It's very much my business. In fact, I think you were actually drawing *my* business. Was that a swimming pool you were drawing?"
"No." She cracked a smile. "I was just drawing water."
I scowled.
"Water inside four walls!" I said, accusatorily. She started giggling. "In a backyard! With a diving board!" By now she was laughing uncontrollably.

"Let me see that!" I reached for her sketchbook. She pulled it away from me, but as she did that, a bunch of papers went flying into the air. And there it was. One of her drawings floated slowly down to the ground and when it landed I could see it, clear as day. Not just a swimming pool, but in bright orange big letters it said Pool Cleaning Service.

"Addison!" I shouted. "What are you doing?!"

"It's called marketing," she said in the voice of a grown-up, tired of explaining the same thing over and over again to a child.

"You don't even know what that is!"

"Yes I do," she huffed. "Dad told me what it means."

"Oh yeah, well what is it?"

"I am making flyers to promote my pool cleaning business."

"You don't have a pool cleaning business!" I stomped my foot. "I do."

"Not yet, I don't, but I expect that soon I will."

I looked down again at the flyer she had drawn. There was a phone number on it. I pointed to it.

"Mom said I could use her number," she said.

I was about to tell her this whole thing was crazy, it would never work. But I was stopped short in my tracks. I do believe my jaw was open. I might have even been drooling, if you want to know the truth.

"Addie!" I gave her a big hug. "This is a great idea! That's exactly what I need to find new customers."

"But you don't know how to draw."

"Yes I do," I said defensively.

"No, you don't," she smirked. "Even your stick figures don't look like sticks, they look like nervous spaghetti."

"You have a point. Maybe you can draw them for me."

"No thanks," she said and quickly picked up her papers and started to head out of the kitchen.

"Wait! Addie wait!"

"I'll pay you."

"How much?"

"I don't know. A dollar."

"No way,"

"Two dollars?" I said hopefully.

She shook her head

"Three?"

"Half."

"A half dollar?" I giggled. "Ok, sure."

"No, I want half of everything you make cleaning pools."

"What?!" I shrieked.

"That's right, 50-50."

"No way, not a chance! Get lost."

"Ok," she said in that *you're-going-to-regret-this* tone of voice and started to walk away.

I swallowed. There was something stuck in my throat. Ok, you might even say it was pride. I swallowed my pride and called out, "Addie! Come back."

"Yes, brother?" she teased.

"I'll give you a third."

She pretended to think about it, and then said, "No."

"Forty percent."

"No."

"Forty! Addie, that's a lot."

"I don't want forty, I want to be your partner. An equal partner."

"My partner?" I said sarcastically.

"That's right. Your partner."

"But you don't know anything about cleaning pools. And you're too little to carry heavy buckets of wet leaves."

"And you don't know how to draw. And it sure doesn't seem like you know much about marketing either."

"You want me to give you half of my business just because you can draw flyers? That hardly seems fair. I can get anyone to draw pictures of a pool for me."

"It's not just drawing, Chance. It told you, it's called marketing. I have Mom's phone ready to go, so we can take calls. I made a map of the neighborhood so we can write down which houses we visited and left flyers with, and what they said. I'll find us new customers, if you make me your partner."

I scratched my head. There was something appealing about what she was proposing. It was no fun knocking on doors all day in the hot sun, hoping someone needed their pool cleaned. "Ok, ok. Maybe we can do half of any new customer you bring."

"No," she said. "I want to be a full partner in the whole business, or I'm not interested."

What was up with her? Since when did she negotiate like...Dad. Dad! DAD!!!

"Did Dad put you up to this?"

"No."

"Are you sure? Because it sure seems like it."

"He just gave me some advice, that's all." She smiled.

"No fair." I fumed.

"He said it was pro...probo...no....banana...probanana consulting or something like that."

I was too busy doing math in my head to ask her what the banana meant. Right now between Dad's pool and Larry's, I was making $40 per week, assuming everything worked out with Larry. Now if I made Addie my partner and she didn't bring in any new customers, I'd have to share the $40 with her, which meant I'd only be making $20 per week. My earnings would be cut in half. That's a big risk. But if her flyer could bring in at least one new customer, then we'd be making $60 per week, so my share would be $30. Still not $40. Now if she got two new customers, then we'd be making $80 per week and I'd get $40. Same as now. So two new customers was what Addie needed to bring to make up for the money I'd lose sharing my earnings with her. Dad told me that's called the break-even point. But that's a lot of hassle just to break even. She'd have to bring at least three new customers for it to be worth it. With three new customers we'd have five total, which would be $100 per week and I'd pocket $50. That would be nice. Better than $40.

2 Customers = $40 per week
By myself = $40 per week
With a partner = $40 / 2 = $20 per week

3 Customers = 3 x $20 = $60 per week
With a partner = $60 / 2 = $30 per week
$30 per week with a partner < $40 per week by myself

4 Customers = 4 x $20 = $80 per week
With a partner = $80 / 2 = $40 per week
$40 per week with a partner = $40 per week by myself

5 Customers = 5 x $20 = $100 per week
With a partner = $100 / 2 = $50
$50 per week with a partner > $40 per week by myself

"I figured it out," I said. "We can be partners if you bring in three or more new customers."
She looked at me quizzically. "If I have to go out and get three new customers on my own, which is more than you have now, I might as well just do this myself." She folder her arms and stared right at me. "We're either equal partners or we're not partners at all."
Why did it feel like I was negotiating with my father?
"Your choice, Chance." She said my name emphatically. She'd definitely gotten advice from Dad. "Take a chance on me...or don't. Your choice." She picked out one of her drawings from the sketchpad and held it up. There it was, not just in big orange colors but outlined in glitter too: Addie's Pool Cleaning Service.
"Let me think about it," I said. "It's a big decision."

"Ok. But I want to know by tomorrow. Because if not, I need to get going with these flyers."

"You're really going to do this on your own?"

"Yes, if you won't take me as your partner. Then I'll do it myself." She'd most definitely been talking to Dad. "Ok, fine. You'll have my answer tomorrow."

I spent the rest of the day distracted. No matter what I was doing, all I could think about was Addie's offer. Should I taker her on as a partner?

What would *you* do?

Would you take on a new partner? Why?

What would the benefit be?

Would there be any drawbacks?

Chapter 6

Pros and Cons

It was morning and I still hadn't made a decision. I knew Addie needed an answer, but I was torn. I couldn't figure out if it was a good idea to become partners, so I decided to write down the pros and cons. My dad taught me that one time. I took a sheet of paper and traced a line down the middle. At the top of the left column I wrote down Cons and underlined it. At the top of the right side I wrote down Pros and also underlined it.

I started with the cons. Those were easy. Number One, she was my sister. Who wants to work with their sister? Sisters are annoying. At least mine was. Ever since I can remember Addie always wanted to do whatever I was doing. Second, she probably couldn't help much with the actual pool cleaning. She was never one to get dirty or do her chores willingly. I couldn't imagine her spending a couple hours in the hot sun carrying a heavy net and pulling dead leaves out of the water.

Number Three and, actually, most importantly, I could lose half of my money. If Addie's scheme didn't bring in any new clients, then I would give up half of my pool earnings for nothing. Number Four, that wasn't fair. I mean it really, really wasn't fair.

I tried to think about why the unfairness bothered me so much. It was more than just having to split the money with her. This business was *mine*. I had started it. Sure, it had only been five weeks, but still. I had done a lot of work to get to that point. Not just cleaning Dad's pool, but negotiating, going out and finding another customer. This was something I was building, all by myself. I didn't like the idea of sharing, of giving part of it up to someone else. I liked being able to say to myself this was all mine. All of it. I didn't want to give that up.

I smiled, satisfied with myself. I tried to think of more cons, but no other ones came to mind. But those were enough. I had five really good reasons not to make Addie my partner. So I turned my attention to the right side of the sheet, the pros. Those were a lot harder to come up with. I stared at the white sheet for a long time. All I could think about was how I would lose half of my money and how that wasn't fair. Not fair at all!

Finally I forced myself to concentrate. I had to admit her flyers looked nice. She did a good job with them. And she was right, I couldn't draw. Nobody wants to look at doodles of nervous spaghetti. That wasn't my strength, but it was something she was good at. So I wrote that down. Maybe she would be better at finding customers than I was. Maybe she wouldn't be, but did I want to take that risk? If I didn't agree to make her my partner, she'd be out there slipping flyers under the same doors I was knocking on. Our neighborhood was only so big. Could it support two different kids offering a pool cleaning service? Maybe it would be good to partner with her just to keep her from competing with me.

As I thought about it, I also had to admit she had good ideas. This whole marketing thing was a new concept I hadn't really thought of. It definitely solved the two problems I was worried about before. If we could leave a flyer describing our pool cleaning business at each house, then it didn't matter if they were home or not. They could read it whenever they got home. If they didn't have a pool they could just throw the flyer away. But if it was me knocking on doors though, I would have to waste twenty minutes talking to them, like I did with the nice old lady who gave me candy and the pimply teenager who wanted to steal my idea. On the other hand, if they did have a pool, maybe they'd look at the flyer and decide to call. In that case I'd be happy to go talk to them about our service and how we guarantee not just a clean pool, but peace of mind too.

*Look at that! I just said **our** cleaning service, and they would call **us**.* What was wrong with me? Was I forgetting how unfair this all was? Then I remembered that Addie got Mom to let her use her phone number. She *was* always good at getting Mom and Dad to help her. Ok, if I really thought about it, she was better at asking for help than I was. I usually had a lot of pride to swallow, but she didn't seem to have that problem.

I tried to think if there were other pros. I remembered something my mom had told me once, she said two were better than one. Maybe this is what she meant. I was good at cleaning pools, negotiating, talking to customers, figuring things out. Addie was good at art, coming up with new ideas —she was very creative I had to admit—, and asking for help. Maybe it was true, two were better than one, and together we could do more things, in different ways, and do them better, than we could if each of us were on our own. This way I could focus on what I did best, and have her do the things I really didn't enjoy doing.

There was something else. I could trust Addie. Sure, she was annoying sometimes. But she's still my sister. She wouldn't intentionally try to mess me up or run off with all my money. It's true I could probably find someone else to draw the flyers and just pay them for it without giving up half my business. But they wouldn't be a partner. Not like Addie would. Someone who really cared if we succeeded or failed, and someone I could trust to have our best interests at heart.

I wrote down one more pro. If Addie's plan did work, there was the chance that we could make a lot more money than I could if it was just me. This whole time, I had kept thinking about what would happen if Addie's flyers didn't get us any new customers, or only got us one or two. But what if her marketing got us three customers, or five, or even 10. That would be amazing!

Was that a chance worth taking? I turned the paper over and drew two lines across, so I divided the page into thirds. At the top of the first section, I wrote down Worst Possible Outcome. That was easy, I quickly scribbled: "0 new clients. Result = $20 a week instead of $40."

CONS	PROS
1. She's my sister and she can be annoying.	1. She can draw and make nice flyers.
2. She can't really help clean.	2. Remove a competitor.
3. I could lose half my money.	3. She has some good ideas.
4. It isn't _fair_!	4. She knows how to ask Mom & Dad for help.
5. It would no longer be all mine. I'd have to share control.	5. Two are better than one.
	6. I can trust her.
	7. If her marketing works we could get a lot more customers.

Below that I wrote Normal Outcome. I had to believe that, over time, with Addie's help and with her flyers, we could get at least two more customers, which is what we have now. *Aargh why did I keep saying* **we** *again?* So in that case, I'd be making $40 dollars a week, just like I am now. That seemed very reasonable. This was the most likely result.

And then at the bottom of the page I wrote down Best Outcome. Let's say Addie got us four more customers. That would be six total. Then we'd be making $120 per week, and I'd get half of that, $60 a week. Plus that seemed a lot more stable. What if Larry changed his mind? Then I'd be back to just cleaning Dad's pool. But if we had six customers, losing one of them wouldn't be as big a deal.

I glanced back up at the worst possible outcome I had written down. I scratched my head. Would I be ok if the worst happened? Yes I would. I could handle it. Now it would be a bummer to only make $20 each week, but not the end of the world. It would take me twice as long to get Midnight Blue, but other than that, not that big of a deal. On the other hand, the best possible outcome…well that made me giddy to think about. I realized I had spent all my time thinking about the worst possible outcome and not enough thinking about the best possible outcome.

Then I had another thought. Summer was almost halfway done. I was nowhere close to my goal of making $225 to buy Midnight Blue. If I was going to make it, I had to do something different. I had to be true to my name and take a chance.

I put the pencil down. I had one more thing to think about. This wasn't only about Addie. This was about me, and what I wanted. What did I really hope for? Did I dream about scooping up dead leaves and drowned insects? Not really. I was already kind of getting bored with that. But what I did daydream about, what I fantasized about, was running a business. A real business. I had been having fun ever since Dad put that idea of leverage in my head. I like a challenge. And, I have to admit, again, Addie's flyers had inspired me to dream big. I imagined us running a real company with lots of customers. That was easier to do with a partner. Even if there were just two of us struggling to find another customer, that felt like we were a real business, building a dream. When it was just me, it was hard not to feel like I was just cleaning pools.

Worst Possible Outcome
0 new customers
$40 per week from existing customers
My share = $40 / 2 = $20 per week

Normal Outcome
2 new customers
$40 from new + $40 from existing = $80 per week
My share = $80 / 2 = $40 per week = same as now

Best Possible Outcome
4 new customers (or more)
$80 from new + $40 from existing = $120 per week
My share = $120 / 2 = $60 per week or more

I flipped the paper over and circled the Pros at the top of the right column. And then I went to go look for Addie. She was in the kitchen eating cereal. She didn't even look up, but she did mumble, "Good morning, Chance."

"Good morning partner!" I said very enthusiastically.
"Really?" She looked at me half expecting me to say I was joking.
"Really." I stuck my hand out to shake hers. She was still skeptical. Her hands hung at her side. So I reached over, grabbed her right hand, and started shaking it anyway.
"I'm serious Addie. I thought about it, and I think we'll make a good team."
"Oh wow! That's so great."
"There's just one condition."
"Chance!" she cried out, disappointed.
"No, listen, Addie. It's not so bad. I'll give you half of everything from

now on. We'll be true partners, just like you want. But I get to keep the money I've made so far. It's only fair." I had been cleaning pools for five weeks by then and had earned $50, now that Dad was paying $20 per cleaning.

She looked like she was about to complain, but she stopped herself. Then she gave me a big hug and started to run away.

"Where are you going?"

"I've got to go change the flyers, and put your name on them too," she said hurriedly as she scampered off. "There's no time to waste. Bye!"

I grinned. Then I sat down to finish eating the bowl of cereal she had started. I started to wonder, what did it mean to have a partner? What would be different now? What would change?

What do *you* think?

How would things be different with a partner?

What adjustments would you have to make?

Chapter 7

Powerful Brain Waves

The following Tuesday I was at Larry's house at the scheduled time to clean his pool. I admit I was nervous. It was my first real job, if you don't count cleaning my dad's pool, and I don't. I even got there five minutes early because I wanted to make a good impression.

Just as I was about to knock on the door, it swung open. And there was Larry holding a briefcase. Suddenly I wasn't sure if he remembered me.

"Hello, good morning Larry." He looked distracted and didn't respond right away. "I mean, sir. Good morning, sir...I'm here to clean your pool."
"Yes, yes, of course. The door to the back patio is unlocked, so you can go ahead and do your work. I have to go to a meeting."
"Uh.... Ok." I wasn't sure how to ask, so I just looked at him in kind of a funny way that said, *I hope you can read my mind.*
But he couldn't read my mind.
"Will you be back soon?" I asked.
"No, I'll be out all day."
I tried to send him powerful brain waves so he could read my mind, but it wasn't working.
"Ok thank you, sir."
"Quit calling me sir."
"Yes sir – I mean Larry. Sorry, sir. Larry."
"All right then, I will see you later."
I gave him one last pleading look.
"Oh! I almost forgot. I left your money on the kitchen counter."
"Thank you!" Maybe he *could* read my mind after all, only there was just a bit of a delay in my powerful brain waves reaching him. "Thank you Sir Larry!"

He looked at me with a furrowed brow and then started laughing.
"Sir Larry it is then."
"Thank you Larry! I mean, Sir Larry."
"You're welcome. And I'll see you again next week, same time."
"Yes! Great! Thank you."

I said goodbye to Larry and headed through the living room towards the door that led to the back patio where the pool was. I opened the door and set down the net and bucket I brought with me. I wasn't sure if Larry would have any so I brought mine, just in case. I kept thinking it was a bad idea because the net is pretty heavy to carry, but now I was glad I did. It didn't look like Larry had one and it would've been a disaster to show up without the right tools for the job.

I was about to get started when curiosity got the best of me. I went back inside the house and walked over to the kitchen counter. Sure enough, there was a crisp twenty dollar bill tucked under the coffee maker. I couldn't believe it. I couldn't believe that Larry would trust me like this, take off to go to work and leave me alone in his house, with a $20 bill for work I hadn't even yet done. How did he know I would do it? How did he know I would do a good job? How did he know I wouldn't just take the money and run?

I realized then that Larry trusted me. That was amazing. He didn't really know me, not really. But he believed that I would do a good job. And that made me *really* want to do a good job. I would work extra hard that day, to prove that Larry was right to trust me.

I actually spent three hours cleaning Larry's pool. In part because I was being very careful, going slow to make sure I did a good job. But also because when I was almost done the net broke. The pole cracked in half and it became very difficult to reach the far places with the stump I had left. And there was a bunch of leaves stubbornly floating in the middle of the pool just out of reach. I had to make waves with my hands so that the leaves would eventually drift to the edge of the pool where I could get to them with my broken net.

But all in all it went well. It felt good to do a good job. By the time I went back into the kitchen to retrieve my $20 bill I was very proud of the work I'd done.

The walk back home with a broken net was a real drag. If you think it's hard walking around with a pole that is twice as long as you are, try walking around with two half poles that are each as tall as you are.

When I finally made it home I looked for Addie to tell her the good news that everything had gone well with Larry and we did in fact have him as a client. But she wasn't home. She must've been out with Mom. So I grabbed some iced tea and went to the backyard to kick the soccer ball around.

Dad was the first to get home. I told him all about my adventures at Larry's house. I slowly unfurled the $20 bill I had tucked into my pocket and showed him my very first payment ever from a real customer. He told me he was proud of me and gave me a big high five. That made me happy.

"Oh, I almost forgot," I said. "I need a new net. Ours broke while I was cleaning Larry's pool."
"Good thing you just got paid," my dad said. "You should be able to find a nice net for under $20."
"What!" I exclaimed. "What do you mean?"
"Well you need a good net if you're going to be in the pool cleaning business, right?"
"But...but."
"Yes?" My dad raised an eyebrow dramatically. I hate when he does that.
"Well...well, I guess I just assumed you'd buy another one."
"Oh I will," my dad said.

Whew. That was close. "I thought you meant that I had to buy it."

"I'm buying a new net for *our* pool, but you need to buy one for *your* pool cleaning business."

"What? Why can't I just use yours?"

"Because I don't want to have to keep buying a new net every time it breaks while you're cleaning somebody else's pool."

"But—"

"If you're going to have a pool cleaning business, you need to buy your own equipment."

"But those cost money. A lot of money!"

"Good thing you're making $20 every time you clean a pool," my dad smirked.

"But why does that mean I have to buy my own equipment?"

"You were the one who said you wanted to be an *official* vendor, remember?"

"Yeah..."

"Well a vendor has his own on equipment and tools to do the job."

So this is what my dad meant. I have to admit, I did not see this coming. "But I don't want to spend all my money on nets and buckets!"

"You don't have to spend all your money, just some of it. If you want to have a business, then you have to make some investments. Spend money now on tools, so you can do more jobs and make even more money later. That's how it works."

"Oh."

"Or do you want to just go back to cleaning our pool for $10?"

"Maybe," I said grumpily. No one said anything about having to buy equipment.

"It's up to you, Son."

"Maybe I don't want to make investments," I cried out. "I'm just trying to buy a bike!"

"Sounds like you have some thinking to do, buddy."

"This is harder than I thought," I said. "I don't want to work all summer and at the end all I really have are a couple buckets and nets."

"Well then you need to track your expenses carefully and keep an eye on your bottom line."

"My bottom what?"

"Your bottom line," my dad said. "Your profits."

"What's that?"

"Well your top line is the money you get from doing these jobs. It's your revenue. And from that you have to subtract your expenses. What's left at the bottom is the money you get to keep. That's your profit."

"Why can't I just keep all the money at the top?"

"Because money doesn't grow on trees."

"No, but it does grow in my dad's wallet."

He laughed. "I wish Son. I have to do the same thing, keep an eye on our expenses and make sure we're spending less than we make. I will buy a net for our family pool from my top line and you'll buy a net for your cleaning business from yours."

"I need to think about this," I said defiantly. "Maybe I have no business being in business. Maybe I should just spend my summer playing soccer and eating ice cream."

"Maybe," my dad said. And then he picked up the newspaper and resumed reading.

I went back to my room and started thinking. I took out the money I had stashed away in my sock drawer and counted it. I had exactly $70.00, including the $20 Larry just gave me. I'd been cleaning pools for five and a half weeks. The first four weeks I got paid $10 but I spent all my money the first week, before I decided to start saving up for Midnight Blue. So I had $30 from the second, third and fourth weeks, and then $20 from the week after my dad agreed to pay $20 to clean the pool. And now I had the $20 Larry had just paid me.

I took out a notebook and wrote down Revenue and next to it: $70. Below that I wrote Expenses and then started a list: Net $14. I wasn't sure how much they cost but $14 seemed like a good guess. And then I wrote down, Bucket $4.

I subtracted my expenses from my revenue and wrote down my profit, which would be $52. And then I remembered. I had agreed to split any new earnings with Addie. That wouldn't leave me with much, if I decided to buy a net and a bucket.

I looked at the crisp $20 bill that Larry had left on the counter for me. Then I calmly unfolded all the other dollar bills and stacked them on top of the $20 bill. I don't think I'd ever had that much money in my hands at once. I was very tempted to just call it a day, and not buy another bucket. Tell Addie I was out, she could keep the business and I would keep my $70. How much ice cream could $70 buy? I would like to find out. I'm sure it's a lot.

Revenue
Dad Pool Cleaning $50
Larry Pool Cleaning $20
Total Revenue: $70

Expenses (estimated)
Net $14
Bucket $4
Total Expenses: $18

Profit
Revenue – Expenses: $52

I stared at the stack of money for a long time, trying to decide if I should stay in business or not. If I had to buy my own net, who knows what other expenses would come up? Did I really want to do this? Was it worth it?

What would *you* do?

Would you spend the money on new equipment?

What's the benefit of making that investment? What's the downside?

Chapter 8

Running Out Of Crayons

I decided to stick with it. I just needed some time to think about it and get a better perspective. I realized I'd worked too hard to let something like having to buy my own equipment stop me.

I also realized that the eighteen or so dollars I would have to spend on the net and bucket seemed like a lot because so far I had only made seventy dollars. And $18 feels like a huge chunk of $70. And that's because it is: $18 is 25.7% of $70. But then I realized something else. Hopefully the net and bucket would be a one-time expense. So over time, as I cleaned more pools and made more money, my expenses as a portion of my revenue would keep getting smaller.

I only had to wait a couple more days before I would get to clean Dad's pool, and get paid $20 by him. So then my total revenue would be $90. Which means that the $18 in equipment costs would only be 20.0%.

And if I waited just one more week, and cleaned both Larry's pool and Dad's pool, I would bring in another $40. So my little company's revenue at that point would be $130 and our $18 of expenses would represent 13.8% of the total. That's much better. Fourteen percent is almost half of twenty-six percent. My revenue would keep growing but my expenses would stay the same, at least for a while. So as a percentage of the total, they would keep getting smaller.

It got even better a month out. After four more weeks of cleaning both Dad and Larry's pool, making $20 each time, I would have $210. And it's not like I'd have to buy a new net and bucket each time. At that point, the $18 I'd had to spend to get my own tools and be a real business would only be 8.6% of my revenue. That was much more reasonable.

Revenue: $70
Estimated Expenses: $18
18 / 70 = 0.2571
Estimated Expenses As Percent of Revenue = 25.7%

Revenue: $90
Estimated Expenses: $18
18 / 90 = 0.2000
Expenses % Revenue = 20.0%

Revenue: $130
Estimated Expenses: $18
18 / 130 = 0.1384
Expenses % Revenue = 13.8%

Revenue: $210
Estimated Expenses: $18
18 / 210 = 0.0857
Expenses % Revenue = 8.6%

Maybe this is what Dad meant when he said I had to invest money in the beginning to make even more money down the road. I didn't want to admit it to my dad, but math was really helping me. I could calculate numbers into the future, like how much I expected to make and earn, and that made it easier to make big important decisions today about tomorrow.

I went to go look for my dad. He was in the garage trying to fix an old radio. It's a hobby of his. He likes buying up vintage radios from when he was a kid and restoring them.

"Dad, I'm ready to buy the tools I need to run my own pool cleaning business."
"Are you sure, Son?"
"Yes, I thought about it overnight and I thought about what you said. I'm ready to make an investment. Can you drive me to the store?"
"Happy to." He set his tools down, put a hand on my shoulder and said, "Proud of you, Son."

It turned out the net was actually $15.99 and the bucket was $4.99. With tax it all came out to $22.55, which was a little more than I had anticipated. That was a bummer, but I reminded myself that what I had figured out still held true. This was a one-time expense that would keep getting smaller as a share of my total revenue the more pool cleaning jobs I completed.

On the way home my dad stopped to get a coffee. I didn't mind because it also meant he got me a root beer float. The float was especially good since I hadn't bought any ice cream ever since I started saving up for Midnight Blue.

As we were leaving the coffee shop we ran into someone Dad knew. They chatted for a little bit until he remembered I was there.
"Son, this is Mr. Dubois."
"Nice to meet you," I said without taking my eyes off the blob of vanilla ice cream floating in my cup.
"Mr. Dubois is one of our investors," my dad said.
That got my attention. "Oh, very nice to meet you, sir. My name is Chance." I stuck my hand out to shake his.

"Nice to meet you," he said.

He had large bushy eyebrows that seemed to span the full width of his forehead. I looked closely to see if they were in fact two eyebrows or just one enormous strip of hair. I couldn't quite tell.

"We have high hopes for your father's company," Mr. Dubois added.

"I have a company," I said, forgetting about my root bear float entirely. "Will you invest in it too?"

Mr. Dubois chuckled. "Well that depends, young man. What kind of company is it?"

"A pool cleaning company." I looked over at my dad, who smiled in return.

"Very interesting," he said in a way that didn't sound like he was actually very interested.

"Will you invest in it?"

"How many customers do you have?"

"I just got my second customer," I replied, proudly.

He looked straight at me, frowning. His eyebrows came together aggressively.

"You're not a real company without customers. Talk to me when you have customers."

He and Dad chatted a bit more and then we said goodbye. For some reason, the ice cream in my float didn't taste very good after that. I was too annoyed by what Mr. Dubois had said. How dare he say I didn't have a real company.

When we got home, I went straight to Addie's room and knocked on her door.

"Addie, we need more customers."

"I know," she said. "I've been working on them all day."

"Let me see them."

She was excited to show me. She brought out her sketchpad and started laying out all her drawings on the bed. There were about ten of them.

I had to admit she'd done a good job. She had drawn a pool on each of them, colored it in different shades of blue, and then added a little bit of glitter so that the water looked sparkling clean. She had both our names written across the top. Chance & Addie's Pool Cleaning Service. She used yellows and oranges with the letters outlined in red that kind of looked like a sunrise over a pool.

"Addie! These are great."
"Do you really think so?"
"Yes I do."
She beamed. "Thanks. I've been working hard on these."
"I can tell. Where are the rest of them?"
"What do you mean?"
"Well, I only see..." I started counting "nine...ten...eleven. We need more than eleven."
"These take a long time to make, Chance. I can make two or three, maybe even four a day."
"Four! That's going to take forever."
"How many do we need?"
"At least fifty. That's how many doors I knocked on, but I was hoping we could get a hundred."
"A hundred! I don't think I even have enough crayons to draw a hundred."
"Aargh. Let me think..." *Four new flyers a day...Even if we wait another week, that still only gets us around 30 flyers.* "We need more than that."
"I'll try to draw faster," Addie offered hopefully.
"What can we do, Chance?"
"I don't know." I rubbed my face. "I'm not sure."
She looked at me, worried.

I looked at her. A thought flashed across my mind. Maybe I shouldn't have agreed to be partners with her. Maybe this had been a mistake. Had it really been worth giving up half my business for this?

I was torn. If I was going to drop Addie as my partner, now was the time to do it. Maybe I could just figure out how much money we'd made since I said we could be partners and give her a fair share. And then tell her we're better off each doing our own thing.

What would *you* do?

Would you tell Addie you'd made a mistake agreeing to be partners?

Or would you stick with her? Why?

Chapter 9

Barking Like A Groggy Dog

I tried to remember all the reasons I originally thought it was a good idea to have Addie as my partner. And all the reasons why it wasn't a good idea. But I couldn't concentrate on them. I just kept thinking about how I had already told her we were partners.

I had made a promise to her. That was the real issue. Did I want to break my promise? I have to admit I was tempted.

My dad always warned me it was important to keep my word. But why? I tried to think about why that was important.

And then it occurred to me that if I went back on my agreement with Addie, then maybe Dad could go back on his agreement with me and drop me as his vendor.

Then I imagined Larry changing his mind and randomly deciding to pay less than the agreed amount.

Suddenly nothing felt stable. If I couldn't trust people to do what they said, I couldn't really make any plans without constantly wondering if the other person would come through or not. I didn't want to live like that.

How could I make sure other people kept their promises to me? I couldn't control them. But by being someone who says what he means and sticking to it, I could make it more likely they would treat me the same way.

"Don't worry Addie. We'll figure it out." I pushed aside the thought that had crept in. Addie was my partner. I needed to stick by her. I couldn't think about going back on our agreement every time we hit a rough spot. That wasn't right. This was Addie, my sister. I couldn't do that to her. I had said we would be partners and I needed to keep my word.

"We will?" she asked, hopefully.

"I've got it!" I said excitedly. "I know what we should do."

"You do?" Addie sounded skeptical.

"It's easy," I said, putting my hand on her shoulder. "We'll make copies."

"How?"

"We'll pick your best drawing and go get photocopies made."

"But that costs money."

"Yes, but it's an investment. Don't you see?"

"I thought you didn't want to spend money."

"Addie," I said seriously, "sometimes you have to spend money to make money. Just trust me on this."

"Ok, if you say so."

In fact, I did say so. We picked her best drawing and then asked Mom to drive us to the office store so we could make copies. It was hard to pick, she had lots of great ones. We spent a lot of time deciding. In the end we picked the one where the phone number was the largest. That seemed like a good idea.

Profit & Loss Statement

Dad Pool Cleaning: $70

Larry Pool Cleaning: $20

Total Revenue: $90

Expenses

Net & Bucket $22.55

100 Photocopies $9.68

Total Expenses: $32.23

Profit/Loss

Revenue – Expenses: $90 - $32.23

Profit: $57.77

The copies were nine cents each. We had 100 made. So it cost us nine dollars plus tax, $9.68. When we got home I added it to my profit tracker, which dad explained is called a P&L, or a Profit and Loss statement. This is what it looked like after buying the bucket, the net, and a hundred photocopies.

The next morning we were ready to go. We divided up the flyers. I put my half in an old satchel. Addie put hers in her favorite pink backpack. She even emptied it out beforehand. Colored pencils, gum, a pencil sharpener, a bracelet, tissues, chapstick...all of it came out.

We went to the same neighborhood where I had found Larry a couple weeks back, but chose a different street that ran parallel so we could hopefully reach new customers this time and not duplicate what I'd done before. I took the left side of the street and Addie took the right.

We were moving quickly and efficiently through the street, tucking a folded flyer under each door. I glanced over every once a while to see what Addie was doing. She was working hard and keeping pace with me. It made me happy to see how seriously she was taking it.

I was almost out of flyers when I heard Addie screaming. I turned around and saw her running frantically. A big hairy dog was chasing her and barking loudly. It looked mean. Really mean. She started running even faster, cutting across lawns and zigzagging. Flyers were spilling out of her backpack. She even hurdled over a hedgerow. But it didn't matter, the dog was closing in on her fast.

Instinctively I started running towards the dog and barking as loud as I could. It didn't seem to notice me, so I started barking louder and louder and running faster and faster. It finally noticed me – just in time because he was almost at Addie's legs. The dog turned around and, before I had time to react, leaped at me, crashing into my chest and knocking me down. I tried wrestling the beast off of me, but he was heavier than I thought. I just remember his hot breath on my face and some of his spittle dripping down on me.

I thought I was doomed for sure.

"Milton!" I heard a voice shout out. "Milton! Stop it!"
And just like that the dog jumped off me and sat on his hind legs, just like you would expect a dog to sit in obedience school.
"Bad Milton! Bad, bad, bad!"
Milton whined and lowered his head in shame.
"I'm so sorry," a red-haired woman with freckles said. "I'm terribly sorry."
I was too shocked to say anything. Addie ran up panting for breath and managed to blurt out, "Chance! Are you ok?"
"I'm fine." I started to stand up and brush some of the grass off of my shirt.
"Really, truly, I am sorry," the woman said. She sounded like she had a Scottish accent. "He's actually a good dog, just a little over friendly."
"A little?" I said sarcastically.
"I thought he was going to bite me!" Addie exclaimed. "So I started running."
"Oh no," the freckled woman laughed. "Milton just wants to play."
"Really?" I didn't believe her. "He has a funny way of showing it."
"Really."
I still didn't believe her.
"Go ahead and pet him," she said.
"Uh…no thanks." Having just survived the canine attack, I wasn't about to invite danger again.
"I'll do it!" Addie jumped in and started petting Milton. He started playfully licking her face and she started giggling.
Grudgingly I started to pet him too. He seemed ok.
"Here let me help you, please." The freckled woman started to pick up some of the flyers that Addie had dropped as she was running away. She gathered them up in a pile and then handed them to me.

56

Then she took one and started to read it.

"You guys clean pools?"

"Trying to," I said.

"I have a pool."

"You do?"

"Yes, and I hate cleaning it."

"We can take care of that."

"Splendid. Can you come on Monday?"

"Certainly!"

"Great. My name is Elspeth. And you've already met Milton."

"I'm Chance." I reached out my hand to shake hers. "This is Addie. And we'll do a great job cleaning your pool."

That night at the dinner table Addie told the story of how I saved her life.

"...so then he started running out into the street and barking like a dog!" Addie waved her arms. My parents laughed. So did my little sister.

"Like a dog!" she continued. "He didn't yell like a human. He barked like a dog. He sounded like someone had just stepped on his tail." Addie imitated my panicked barking. And then she laughed. Loudly.

"No, no, it was more like a dog had just taken too much cold medicine and was barking kind of groggily."

My parents guffawed. Even my baby brother started laughing, though I doubt he understood what was so funny. He was imitating my parents and his sisters.

"No, wait, it was both. He barked like a dog who's tail had been stepped on after sneaking into the medicine cabinet and drinking a bottle of cough syrup." Then Addie barked. "Aoouuu! Aoouu! Like that!"

I couldn't help but laugh too.

As we were clearing dishes my mom reminded me of the big game. "Amit is coming by tomorrow to pick you up at 9. His mom will take you guys to the stadium," she said.

Amit is my best friend.

"Awesome! I can't wait to see the Warriors in action. They need to win to make it to the playoffs. I hope they score lots of goals."

I had totally forgotten about the game and got really excited.

"Don't you have something to do tomorrow morning?" my dad asked.

Yikes! Tomorrow was Friday and I had promised to have the pool cleaned by noon each Friday.

"Dad, is it ok if I skip the cleaning tomorrow and do it on Saturday?"

He frowned.

"Please? The playoffs are coming up. And Sandro's red hot, he's scored two goals in the last game. If he gets hot again and scores, we've got a chance."

"Our deal is that the pool is clean by noon every Friday."

"Just this once, Dad. Please!"

"I may have to find a different pool cleaning company."

"What?" That caught me by surprise.

"You were the one that said you wanted me to treat you like an official vendor, remember?"

"I know, but that was then. That was before I remembered the big game. I had totally forgotten, or I would have cleaned the pool today."

"You made a commitment, Son."

"I know," I said quietly. "But I really want to go to the game."

"Sounds like you need to decide what's more important. Going to the game or honoring the commitment you made?"

I was stunned quiet.

"Sometimes you have to make sacrifices if you're going to run a business."

"I don't want to make sacrifices. I want to see Sandro score goals."

"You need to think very carefully about this."

It was true. I did need to think about this. As much as I liked making money from cleaning pools, I liked the Warriors even more. Plus, I had told Amit that I could go to the game. I didn't want to let him down either. What should I do? Should I stick with my commitment to clean the pool, just like any *official* vendor would? Or should I just skip out on it, and go to the game?

What would *you* do?

Would you go to the game or clean your dad's pool?

What's more important? Why?

Chapter 10

A Brilliant Idea

Of all the decisions I had to make to get KidVenture off the ground, that one might have been the hardest. I was really torn. I really wanted to go to the game. I hadn't seen the Warriors play in person at the stadium all season. I had been so excited a month prior when Amit had invited me. He loves soccer just as much as I do, if not more. In fact, that's probably why we're best friends. He had invited me just before I started cleaning pools, which suddenly felt like a long time ago. Back then, I could barely contain my excitement and I couldn't imagine *not* going to the game.

But so much had happened since then. That's why I was so torn. I had worked hard to get to this point with the pool cleaning business. Part of me wondered why my dad couldn't just let it go and let me clean the pool on Saturday so I could go to the game. But deep down I knew the reason. He kept calling it character. "It's building character Son," he would say anytime there was something hard I didn't want to do. I always wanted to talk back and say, "Just how much character do I need? Don't I have enough already?" But I knew better.

I knew what my dad would say. I could even hear his voice in my head so clearly. Of course I could go to the game, it was my decision to make. But I had to understand what it meant. Sometimes in life there are choices, and there's no escaping it. You have to choose one thing, which means giving up the other thing. I could go to the game, but that meant our pool wouldn't be clean by noon on Friday, which was my agreement with Dad. And it wasn't really about whether the pool would be clean at the exact time I had promised. In fact, I can only think of one time my dad actually swam in the pool all summer. It was about keeping my promises, it was about taking my commitments seriously. It was a test to see how serious I was about this new business. And the only way to know, would be to see if I was willing to choose it over something I really liked. Like seeing Sandro score a goal from an angle shot at the corner of the box, just as I had imagined so many times when I myself was taking an angle shot in my back yard, pretending to be the new star striker of the Warriors.

I must've spent hours trying to decide what to do, or at least it felt like hours. Like I said, sometimes in life there are choices to be made, and there's no escaping the fact that to pick one option is to give up the other.

But would you believe it? This was not one of those times. Addie came into my room and saw me slumped against the wall between my bed and dresser, my head hung low.

"Chance," she said, nudging me. "Chance you can go to the game."
"I don't think so Addie, I'm not sure that's a good idea. I think Dad's actually serious about this whole official vendor thing."
"Oh I know he is. You know how Dad gets," she said sympathetically.
"Yep," I said dejectedly. "But I also don't want to let Amit down."
"Well you don't have to."
"What do you mean?"
"I have a solution."
"You do?"
"I'll clean the pool tomorrow."
"You will?" It actually hadn't even occurred to me. Addie wasn't big on manual labor or doing chores. Mom was always on her case about cleaning her room and picking up her dirty clothes, which seemed like a hopeless task. But ask her to draw something, and Addie was on it. I just couldn't picture her spending a few hours in the hot sun cleaning the pool.

61

"Yes Chance, I will. So you can go to the game, and we meet our commitment to Dad, and he keeps us as his pool cleaning service. His *offfffficial* pool cleaning service."

We both started laughing.

"You would do that?" I sat up hopefully.

"That's what partners are for, right?"

I smiled wide. "Right."

"Partner?" She held out her hand to shake mine. She was copying my move.

"Partner." I gave her a firm shake.

Everything was going great. The game was awesome. Sandro scored two goals. The last one was unbelievable. It was in stoppage time with both teams tied 1 to 1. And the Warriors really needed a win to keep their playoff hopes alive. During the last few minutes, everyone attacked, even the goalie. The whole stadium was on its feet. The Warriors forced a corner kick, and Sandro almost scored, but the other team's goalie was really good and knocked the ball out. Another corner kick, another great shot by Sandro, and another amazing save. We were five minutes into stoppage time. I was sure the ref would whistle the game over at any moment. Incredibly, the Warriors got one more corner kick, and this time Sandro didn't miss. Final score: 2-1. Amit was beside himself screaming with joy as we both jumped up and down, giving each other lots of high fives.

I would've been so bummed to miss the game, knowing it had been such an amazing ending. I was so thankful to Addie, really happy she was my partner. I asked her how the pool cleaning had gone, and she held up a $20 bill and smiled proudly.

"Great job Addie!"

"I'm really sore today." She stretched out her arms. "It's hard work cleaning a pool. That net and bucket get heavy after while."

"Yes they do."

"I think I'll stick with marketing and drawing."

"You keep finding us customers like Elspeth and it's a deal."

Speaking of Elspeth, the following Monday I went to clean her pool. Everything went very smoothly. She was super nice, and kept giving me orange juice. I think she still felt bad that Milton had knocked me over and scared Addie. After my third glass of orange juice, I told her not to worry about it. We were definitely even now. And she was right, Milton was actually a very friendly dog. He even jumped in the pool and swam around while I scooped up leaves, which made the time go faster. When he got out of the pool, he went straight to Elspeth and shook his body vigorously to dry off, getting her pretty wet.

"Milton!" She started laughing. She turned to me and said, "He always does that. Big dog just loves attention."
I smiled back.
"Come here you big wet dog. That's right, you're a big wet dog," she said in a playful voice as she started petting him. She didn't seem to mind she was wet. Probably because it was so hot. Did I mention it was really hot that summer?

When I got home, I showed Addie the money. Elspeth had paid me with two $10 bills, which felt like a lot of money. It was our tradition now, I'd show Addie the money, she'd write it down in the ledger we borrowed from Dad, and then we would put it in an old piggy bank I still had sitting around.

The next day I was off to clean Larry's pool, and we did it all over again. Addie wrote down $20 in our revenue column. I have to say, I was pretty impressed. We had three clients paying us $20 every week to clean their pool. The summer was almost two-thirds of the way over, and I would've never imagined at the beginning of summer that I would have a pool cleaning business, three customers, and a business partner. Life was good.

But then a few more days went by, a whole week when we didn't hear from anyone else, and I started to worry. We had passed out a hundred flyers, and only gotten one new customer. And that was Elspeth. And if Milton hadn't gone charging after Addie, who knows if we'd even have her as a client. Maybe she just hired us out of guilt. I started to feel less optimistic. I had knocked on fifty doors and got one customer the first time, and it hadn't cost me any money, just my time. Now we had spent nine dollars to get a hundred copies of Addie's drawing made. And we had spent two hours going house to house, slipping them under the door. And all we had to show for it was Elspeth. I thought things were going to get easier, not harder.

When I did the math, I only became more pessimistic. The first time I went knocking on doors to look for a client, I went to 50 houses and found one client, Larry. That was a 2% success rate. And I thought that was bad. But it had been a week since Addie and I distributed the flyers and out of 100 we tucked into houses, we had only one client, Elspeth. That worked out to a 1% success rate.

Addie's flyers were supposed to improve our success rate, not make it worse. I was feeling down. To distract myself, I leafed through a stack of my dad's old newspapers, turning to the sports section to read about the Warriors game. Something caught my eye. For the most recent game I had been to, the Warriors had 13 shots on goal. Two of those went in. I did some math and figured out that worked out to a 15.3% success rate. That's very different than what I could do by myself in my backyard, where I would shoot and make 66% of all my shots. Obviously it was different shooting in the middle of a Warriors game where the other team has defenders and a goalie trying to stop you. The reality of playing in a real game is very different than just pretending to be in a game in your own backyard.

Take 100 shots on goal in backyard
Make 65 goals
65 / 100 = 65% success rate

Warriors take 13 shots on goal during game
Make 2 goals
13 / 2 = 15.3% success rate

Knock on 50 doors
Get 1 new client
1 / 50 = 2% success rate

Distribute 100 flyers
Get 1 new client
1 / 100 = 1% success rate

Then I remembered the last five minutes of the game. Sandro had three different runs at the goal in those last five minutes. And he didn't give up when he missed the first two. That's what I liked about him. Everyone else on the team was probably thinking the situation was hopeless. But not Sandro. He kept trying and trying.

I decided I wasn't going to give up. I was nowhere close to being done taking my shots on goal. I had to find a way to score when hope seemed lost, just like Sandro did.

I caught a lucky break the very next day. I was in my room when Mom came running in and said there was someone on the phone who was calling about our pool cleaning service. She wanted to know where Addie was. But Addie was out with Dad running errands so Mom handed me the phone. It was a woman named Francine, who told me she'd gotten our flyer and meant to call earlier, but she had misplaced it and finally found it again. She wanted to know how soon we could be there to clean her pool.

"I can be there in a half an hour," I said enthusiastically.
"Great," she responded. "That's perfect."
"I promise we'll do a great job."
"Great. Just one more question."
"Sure."
"How much do you charge?"
I took a deep breath. I suddenly had an idea. This was our chance to make more money. This was our chance to make up for the fact that only one person had responded so far. It was a brilliant idea."
"Thirty dollars. We charge $30."
There was nothing but silence.
The silence grew uncomfortable.
Very uncomfortable.
"We'll make sure your pool is very clean," I said, to say something.
"I don't know, that's too much," she finally answered.
"But—"
"I think I'll have to pass."
"Wait! Twenty-five. We can do it for $25."
"No, thank you. I'll have to think about this."
"Ok, twenty. We can definitely do it for $20."
"But a minute ago you said $30."
"I know. Well..." I stammered. "It's usually $20, but we have a special service ...and I just thought..." I tried to think what I could say to recover, but I was drawing a blank. "It's ok, we'll do it for $20. No problem."
"I don't think so."
"I can be there in half an hour, I just need to get my net and bucket."
"Not today," she said flatly.
"I'll do a good job."
"I'll have to think about it."
"What about next week?"

"I've got to go. Thank you for your time. "
And then the line went dead.

I couldn't believe it. So close. We waited so long for someone to call. And I blew it. It seemed like such a brilliant idea, to ask for more money. An easy way to make an extra $10 per cleaning. But my brilliant idea had turned into a disaster. I felt awful.

Then I thought about Addie and I felt even worse. What was I going to tell her? I had been bugging her, asking her why her flyers weren't working. And now we'd finally gotten a call. And I'd messed it up. I couldn't stand the thought of telling her. Not after being on her case all week.

I tried to think about what to do. Maybe I should just pretend it didn't happen. No wait, that wouldn't work. Mom would tell her about the phone call. Maybe I could tell her the customer just had some questions and wasn't ready to make a commitment yet. That sounded good. Then I wouldn't have to admit I had messed this one up.

I tried to think what the best decision was. Should I tell Addie the truth? Maybe she'd get mad. And then she wouldn't care about working hard anymore. Maybe she wouldn't want to be partners. She could just blame it all on me. Or should I just tell her there was a call but nothing came of it?

What would *you* do?

Would you tell Addie about losing the new client?

Or is it better to pretend it didn't happen?

Chapter 11

Stubborn Weeds

I felt numb. I felt like crawling into bed and hiding under the blankets. I wanted to run away. I wished that phone call had never happened, and I especially wished I had never had that *brilliant* idea. Now I had to either tell Addie that I had messed it all up, or I had to lie to her. I really didn't want to do either.

I tried reading a book to distract myself, but it didn't work. I couldn't concentrate. All I could think about was that Addie would be home soon and I'd have to make a decision one way or another. I felt a knot in my stomach.

Instinctively I went downstairs to look for Mom. I couldn't find her so I checked the backyard. And there she was, working in her garden. She was on her knees down in the dirt, wearing big leather gloves and a big floppy straw hat to protect her from the sun, which was really strong that day. Have I mentioned how hot it was that summer?

I stood there quietly and watched her work for a little bit.

Mom just kept working.

"What are you doing?" I mumbled.
"Pulling weeds." She sat up for a bit, pulled a handkerchief from her pocket, and wiped sweat from her forehead. "Why don't you help me with this one," she said pointing at a prickly yellow weed. "There are some extra gloves in the shed."

I went and got the gloves and then joined my mom down in the dirt. I yanked at the weed. It was a lot harder to pull than I thought. It was such a small little weed on the surface, but apparently it had deep, stubborn roots. I pulled as hard as I could, but I still couldn't get it out of the ground.

"Here, let's try together," Mom said. Then she put her hands on the tuft of the weed and we both pulled at the same time, groaning from the effort. At last it loosened its hold and came out with a jerk, which knocked Mom and me backwards, dirt flying in our faces.

We both stated laughing.

"That was a tough one," Mom said. "Stubborn little creature."
"Sure was."

We kept working. It felt good to be with my mom, even if we didn't say much.

"How did your call go?" she finally asked.
"It went ok, I suppose."

She didn't ask further, just kept working.
Finally, I said, "Not so good actually. I think I kind a messed it all up, but don't tell Addie."
"Hand me the clippers over there," she said. "I need to prune the apple tree."
I reached over and handed them to her.
"I'm sorry about your call."
"It's ok, I suppose." I reached over and held one of the branches for her while she cut it off. "I think I got greedy, asked for too much money and she changed her mind."
It felt good to say it. My mom always had a way to get me to talk.
"That's a tough break, Chance." She put the clippers down and gave me a hug.
"Thanks, Mom."
"I'm sure there will be others."
"That's the only call we've gotten."
"You'll get another chance." She smiled when she said the word chance.

"I hope so. But please don't tell Addie about this."

"Why don't you want to tell her?"

"I don't know." I looked down at my feet and kicked some dirt. "Because she'll get mad?" I said it more like a question.

"Is it because you're afraid of her reaction? Or is it because you don't want to admit to her you were wrong?"

"I don't know." I kicked some more dirt. "Maybe it's both."

"It's ok to make mistakes, Chauncey." My mom used my full name whenever she told me something important. "And it's ok for other people to know you made a mistake."

"I don't want to be criticized, though."

"I know, Son. But you want to be a leader, and being a leader sometimes means you're criticized."

"But if I tell Addie I was wrong, she won't want to follow me anymore."

"Maybe," my mom looked kindly at me. "Or maybe she'll trust you even more because you admit when you're wrong."

"This is hard."

"I know it is. But you're doing a good job. I've been so impressed with how hard you've worked, and everything you've accomplished."

"Thanks, Mom. That's good to hear."

"You will make mistakes. It's part of life. Especially if you set out to do something big like start a business. What matters is how you deal with them."

"What do you think I should do?"

"Well, try to remember what's important. A few weeks from now, whether you got a new client or not isn't really that important. But your relationship with Addie is important. And whether she can trust you is really important."

"I know," I mumbled, and made a halfhearted attempt at kicking up some more dirt.

"She looks up to you, you're her big brother. And you always will be."

"You're right," I grumbled. "I need to tell her."

Later that night I went to Addie's room. She was on her bed drawing. She held up a picture of a sunrise on the ocean.

"Look at this part, right here under the sun," she said excitedly. "I made it a lighter blue, because that's what it looks like when the sunlight is on the water."
"I have something to tell you Addie."
"What?"
"We got a call today, from one of your flyers."
"We did?!" She jumped out of the bed. "Finally!"
"Yes we did, your flyers worked after all."
"That's great!"
"But we lost the customer. I messed it up."
"What?" Her shoulders dropped. Her body looked like a balloon slowly leaking air.
"I'm sorry Addie, I really am."

"What happened?"
"I got greedy, and told her we would clean her pool for thirty dollars and she changed her mind."
"Chance! No. Why did you do that?"
"I made a mistake, Addie."
She curled up her fists and groaned. "Ahhhrrrrgggg!"
"I'm sorry Addie."

There was quiet for a moment. I could hear her breathing. First, loudly and rapidly. Then it got softer and calmer.

"It's ok, Chance."
"What?"
"It's ok."
"It is?"
"You tried. I understand. You were trying to see if you could get us more money."
"Right."
"And it didn't work."
"No."
"Just don't do it again."
"Ok."

And just like that Addie seemed fine. That was my sister. She could get mad really easily, and just as quickly let it go. I wish I could do that.

"I'm sorry I let you down Addie. I know you worked really hard on those flyers."
"It's ok, Chance."
"Really?"
"Yeah, really."
"I thought maybe you wouldn't want to be partners anymore."
"Of course I still want to be partners."
"You do?"
"I love being partners."
"Me too, Addie. Me too."

I went to my room and pulled the piggy bank off my shelf and the ledger from my desk drawer. "Time for a business meeting," I said. "Uh-oh," Addie giggled.

"I'm serious, we are two-thirds of the way through summer. We only have four weeks to go, and I'm still hoping to have Midnight Blue by the first day of school. Let's see where we're at."

We took the money out of the piggy bank and counted it. We added up all our expenses and updated our P&L. We had $190 in revenue and $32.23 in expenses. Our profit so far was $157.77. Fifty of that was all mine, the rest I had to split with Addie. Taking the remaining $107.77 and dividing by two meant that Addie and I each had earned $53.88. So I had $103.88 in total. There was still a long way to go to get to the $225 I needed to buy Midnight Blue. I almost forgot about tax. With tax, the bike would cost $240.75. No wonder I keep forgetting about it. It makes everything harder. I hate tax.

We had three clients: Dad, Larry and Elspeth. We were making $60 a week, $30 each. That meant that over the next four weeks we could expect to make $240. That's assuming we had no new expenses, and we could keep our three existing clients.

Our total projected revenue for the whole summer was $430. That included the $190 we had already made, plus the $240 we were expecting to make over the next four weeks. If our costs stayed the same at $32.23, then our projected profit was $397.77.

That sounds like a lot, but if I subtract the $50 I made on my own before Addie was partner, that only left $347.77 to split between us. My half of that would be $173.88. If I add my $50 back to that, I would have $223.88, not quite enough for Midnight Blue.

And that was only if nothing went wrong and we did keep all our customers through the end of summer. If Elspeth or Larry changed their mind or we somehow missed an appointment, boom that was it. No Midnight Blue. My calculations left us no room for error.

Weeks Left in Summer: 4

Current # of Customers: 3

Project Revenue per Week: 3 x $20 =$60

Projected Revenue Next 4 Week: 4 x $60 =$240

Revenue So Far: $190

Project Revenue Next 4 Weeks: $240

Total Projected Revenue: $430

Expenses So Far: $32.23

Projected Revenue - Expenses: $430 - $32.23

Projected Profit: $397.77

Profit to Split with Partner: $397.77 - $50 = $347.77

Partner's Share of Profit: $347.77 / 2 = $173.88

My total projected earnings: $173.88 + $50 = $223.88

"We need more clients," I said, putting the pencil down.

"I'll make more flyers," Addie offered.

"I don't know, I'm still not sure how well the last ones worked."

"But we got two cust—" Addie cut herself off. "*Almost* two customers."

"That's true, I said. But even if we assume it was two, we could probably get the same amount by knocking on 100 doors. And we wouldn't have to spend nine dollars on printing costs.

"What are you saying? Are you saying we shouldn't do flyers anymore?" Addie looked sad.

"No, I'm saying we need better flyers."
"You don't like my flyers?!" Addie protested.
"It's not that."
"What is it?"
"They seem to be missing something."
"What?"
"I don't know exactly."
"Oh! I know! I'll add more sparkles to them."
"They have enough sparkles. Your flyers are great," I assured her.
 "The artwork is fantastic. I don't think I could find a better artist in the whole city."
Addie beamed.
"But I'm not sure they're saying the right thing. I don't know that they're convincing enough. If they were, we would've gotten a lot more calls."
"So what should they say?"
"I don't know. We need to think about that and figure it out."

So what would *you* do?

How would you make the flyers work better?

How do they need to be different?

Who would you ask for help?

Chapter 12

Banana Consulting

"Dad, I'm ready for some banana consulting."

"Banana consulting?" My dad sounded genuinely perplexed.

"Yeah, I need some of that same banana consulting you gave Addie."

"I didn't give her any bananas."

"Not bananas. Consulting. Pro banana consulting, or something like that."

He still looked perplexed.

"When you gave her advice on marketing."

"Oh!" My dad started laughing. And then he kept laughing and wouldn't stop.

"What's so funny?"

"Now I know what you mean," my dad said, trying to control his laughter.

"What?"

"Pro bono." My dad said the words slowly. "It was pro bono consulting. It has nothing to do with bananas."

"What does pro bono mean?"

"It means for free."

"So you gave Addie advice for free?"

"Of course, I'm her father."

"Well I need some of that free pro bono advice."

"Certainly," Dad said. "But hold on a second. All this talking about bananas is making me hungry." My dad got up from the chair he was sitting in, and moved from the living room into the kitchen. He came back smiling, holding up a banana. He peeled it and started eating.

"Mmm...this is good," he said between bites.

"Dad," I complained. "Come on. This is serious. I need help."

"And this is a *seriously* good banana. Do you want one?" My dad chuckled.

"Come on Dad."

"Sorry, I couldn't help myself." He took the last bite of the banana. "Ok, what do you need help with?"

"My business—our business. Addie and I. We made flyers, and passed them out. But we didn't get the response I thought we would."

"Why do you think that is?"

"I don't know, that's what I'm trying to figure out. I guess they didn't like the flyers. Or at least not enough to call us."

"I think you may be on to something," my dad said. "The flyers need to speak to your target customer, show them you have a solution to their problem, and do it in a language that will persuade them."

"What do you mean?"

"Well you have to talk about things they care about, not so much what you care about."

"How do you know what they care about?"

"Ask."

"Ok." I rolled my eyes. Dad was trying to be funny again. "Dad, what do my customers care about?"

"I don't know. Ask *them*."

"Who?"

"Your customers! Who better to tell you how and why people choose you as their pool cleaning service, than the two customers who actually chose you as their pool cleaning service?"

"You mean Larry and Elspeth?"

"That's exactly what I mean."

"Wow, I hadn't thought about that."

"It's called market research."

"Thanks Dad."

"You're welcome."

I got up to go, but then turned around to ask one more question. "Dad, do you think I was greedy asking for $30 instead of $20?"

"I know you, Chance. You're not greedy. You're a hard worker. You were testing the waters, trying to see what you could charge."

"Did I make a mistake?"

"That depends on what you think a mistake is. You took a risk."

"And it didn't work."

"It wouldn't be a risk if it was always guaranteed to work."

"I feel dumb, because we had a customer and I lost her."

"There's nothing dumb about what you did, Son. It's called price discovery."

"What's that?"

"Well you don't know the true price you can charge until you've tested the market or done your research. You went out and found someone who was willing to pay $20 to have their pool cleaned. And now you found someone who is not willing to pay $30. So It's a good guess that the price the market will support is somewhere between $20 and $30."

"Would you pay $30?"

"No."

"Why not?"

"Well, you do a good job cleaning the pool, removing dead leaves and junk that's landed on the water. But that's all you do. Once you charge $30, I start thinking maybe I'll pay a bit more to a big company and get a full service clean: chlorine refill, floor vacuum, acidity check, and so on. All stuff you don't do."

"I didn't know that."

"Now that you have a real business, it's no longer a simple matter between you and your customer. There are competitors out there fighting for business too."

"So I should just stick to $20?"

"That's up to you, and your appetite for risk. Are you willing to try asking for $30 again, if it means you might lose a customer?"

"Hmm…I don't know." It was a good question. The first few risks I took, asking Larry for $20 and then Dad, had all paid off. But this last one hadn't, and I was wary to try again. "I think I'll just stick to $20 right now."

"Your choice."

"I'd rather get another customer than risk it right now."

"That makes sense."
"Thanks again Dad."
"That'll be $5."
"For what?"
"The consulting."
"I thought banana consulting was free."
"It is free," my dad said. "I'm just messing with you."
"Ok good."
"And it's pro bono consulting, not banana."

I got to Larry's a few minutes early so I could pick his brain. We had a routine now, I would get to his house five minutes early and he would give me any special instructions as he was walking out the door to work.

"Can I ask you a question, Sir Larry?" He was cool with the nickname now. It was easier than always trying to remember not to call him sir.

"Sure thing."

"Why did you pick me to clean your pool?"

"I told you the first day we met. You remind me of my son."

"Hmm, I'm not sure that helps."

"What do you mean?"

"Well, I created some flyers to try to get new customers. But it doesn't seem to be working so well."

"What does the flyer say?"

"It says clean pools, peace of mind, low price of $20." I sang my jingle.

"None of those reasons are why I hired you."

"They're not?" I was surprised to hear him say that.

"No."

"Why not?"

"They sound like any other pool cleaning company, right. There's nothing special about them."

"What?"

I must have looked shocked, because right away he said, "Don't get offended, I mean they're perfectly good selling points. So good, in fact, that you have successfully made yourself sound like a real pool cleaning company."

"But we *are* a real pool cleaning company."

"I know you are." Sir Larry smiled. "But you're not your typical pool cleaning company. At least not one run by adults."

"What's different?"

"If I call ABC pool cleaning company, first I have to talk to a receptionist and schedule a time when someone can come out here. And usually it's a big four hour window so I'm not sure exactly when someone is going to show up, so I have to waste half a day waiting for them. And whoever shows up on one day, may not be the same person who shows up the following week. And they probably don't care about my pool as much as you do. And they're certainly not as friendly. And I guarantee you none of them call me Sir Larry."

We both started chuckling at that.

"So you see, I really did hire you because you remind me of my son. You're a hard-working boy, and I want to support you. You show up when you say you will, and you take pride in what you do."

"I think I'm starting to understand now."

"Don't make yourself sound like a big professional pool cleaning company, because then you're competing with all the other big professional pool cleaning companies. We're deep into summer, I doubt anyone is looking to switch pool companies right now. But there may be more people like me, willing to give a kid like you a chance."

"Wow, that makes sense. Thank you Sir Larry!"

I talked to Elspeth after that and she said many of the same things. She said she liked that I was friendly. I didn't just walk in and start working on her pool without talking to her first. And she really liked that I lived in the same neighborhood, and I was someone she could trust.

"That's important," she said. "If I'm going to let someone into my house, I have to trust them. Even though I do have Milton to protect me."
"I thought you said he was harmless and just wanted to play."
"Oh, he's harmless...if you are." She smiled and called for Milton. "Come here Milton! Where's my harmless big dog? Where's my Milton?"

Milton came running into the room so fast he bumped into a side table, and for a few moments the table lamp on it swayed side to side as if trying to decide whether to topple over or not. Fortunately it didn't.

Elspeth started scratching him behind his ears. "You're a good dog, aren't you Milton? You keep mama safe, don't you?"
Milton barked enthusiastically

Old Selling Points
✓ Clean! Clean! Clean!
✓ Peace of Mind
✓ Low price of $20
✓ Reliability
✓ Promptness

New Selling Points
✓ Pool Cleaning Service Run by Kids
✓ We live in your neighborhood
✓ We'll work hard for you
✓ We're friendly
✓ We'll show up on time

I went home and wrote down everything Larry and Elspeth had said so I could discuss it with Addie. We decided to create a new flyer with our new selling points. Addie was so excited she stayed up late working on the new design and was very proud to show it to me in the morning.

"It looks great Addie. Good job!"
"Thank you, I'm glad you like it."
"Let's go make copies. If you hurry we can ask Mom to drive us."
"How many?"
"A hundred."
"Again? That's a lot of money."
"Yes, we have to try this to see if it will work. We have to take a chance to make money, that's what being an entrepreneur is all about."
"Ok, *Chance*," my sister said sarcastically.
"Dad thinks we might have better luck at Rainbow Ridge. The houses are bigger there, so he thinks more of them probably have pools."
"Let's do it."

Things started to happen very quickly after that. After Mom drove us to the office store to make copies, we turned right around and set out for Rainbow Ridge to pass them out. Mom drove us there too, so we didn't waste any time walking. We got one hundred under doors in an hour and a half. And would you believe it, we got a call that evening from someone wanting us to clean their pool.

Addie was the one to take the call. She was jumping up and down and squealing by the time she hung up.

"We got it, Chance! A new client named Jessica."
"Awesome!" I gave her a high five.
"She wants you there Tuesday at 11:00."

"Cool! No—wait! That's when I clean Larry's pool."

"Oh."

"Can you do it?"

"I'm sorry, Chance. That's when I have my violin lesson." She sounded deflated. "What should we do? Should I call her back and reschedule?"

"No," I said quickly. "I don't want to risk it, not after what happened with Francine."

"Do you want to ask Larry if he'll reschedule?"

"Erg. I'd hate to do that, especially after he was so helpful with our selling points."

"What should we do then?"

"I don't know." I rubbed my face. "Let me think."

So what would *you* do?

Would you ask Jessica if she could pick a different time? Why?

Would you reschedule with Larry?

Is there another solution?

Chapter 13

A Profusely Kind Of Day

"I have a very interesting proposal for you."
"What is it?" asked Amit.
"How would you like to make a little extra money?"
"I'm listening."
"Remember I told you about that pool cleaning business I started."
"Yeah, you told me you were working for your dad and a couple other people for some extra money."
"Well we're growing, and I need help. I have a new client, who wants me to go clean her pool at the exact same time that I'm already scheduled to clean for one of my other clients."
"I can help you."
"Great. I'll pay you."
"Look, you're my friend. If you need help, I will help you out."
"Well it's not just this one time. If all goes well, this might be a regular thing every week. So I'm wondering if I can pay you to clean pools."
"Do you mean work for you?" He sounded kind of surprised.
"Well..." I hesitated, "...not *for* me. With me."
"Who would be my boss?"
"Well..." I hesitated again. I actually hadn't thought about any of this. "I suppose I would."
"Hmm," was all Amit said.
"But, I mean," I tried to think quickly what to say, "we're still friends of course. Best friends. So I'm not really your boss...I'm sure it will be great."
"Ok, I guess I could try it. I could use a little extra money. How much are you paying?"
"How does five dollars an hour sound? You should be able to clean a pool in two hours, so you could make $10 each time."
"And how much do you make?"

"Well…" I *really* hadn't thought about what to say about that. "We charge them $20. So you would be getting half."

"But wait, wouldn't I be doing all the work?"

"Hmm…well, no, not all of it. Addie and I spent two hours putting flyers under people's doors. And we had to design a flyer and pay to print them. And then we had to work things out with the customer. So we're doing plenty of work."

"Ok, I guess I can see that."

"So are you in?"

"Sure, let's try it."

"Great!" I wasn't sure how the conversation would turn out. I was happy he said yes. I gave him all the details: the address, the name of the customer, time of the appointment. I even told him to get there five minutes early, and to try to be friendly.

"Oh! I almost forgot. Do you have a net?"

"A net?"

"Yeah, a swimming pool net, to scoop out the leaves and stuff like that."

"No. Why would I have a net? I don't have a pool, remember?"

"Oh! That's right."

"Maybe I can just use yours."

"Yes, but the whole problem is that I'll be cleaning Larry's pool at the same time. So I'll be using my net and bucket."

"Oh. Well that's no good. I need a net and bucket."

"It's ok. I'll buy another one. In fact, why don't you come over tomorrow and I'll show you how to use it."

"I have used it before, at your house."

"Yeah, but that was just us messing around. Amit, this is serious now."

"Ok, if you say so."

As a matter fact, I did say so, and Amit came over the next day. And I was glad he did, because it turned out I had quite a bit to show him, including how to remove the drain filters and clean them out. I also told him to put all the debris in the bucket and, when it got full, empty it into the big trash bin on the outside of the home.

I realized then, how close I came to making a huge mistake. If I hadn't trained Amit beforehand, it would've probably been a major disaster to send him to a new client. When we were done, I handed him the new net and bucket I had just bought and told him to take it home so he could be ready on Tuesday.

Fortunately it wasn't a disaster, and everything went well that first day. Amit said Jessica had been happy with his work and paid him $20 when he was done. Best of all, she said she wanted him back the following week. So things were looking good.

Profit & Loss Statement

Revenue
Dad Pool Cleaning: $150
Larry Pool Cleaning: $100
Elspeth Pool Cleaning: $60
Jessica Pool Cleaning: $20
Total Revenue: $330

Expenses
Net & Bucket: $22.55 x 2 = $45.10
100 Photocopies: $9.68 x 2 = $19.36
Amit's Wages: $10.00 x 1 = $10.00
Total Expenses: $74.46

Profit/Loss
Revenue – Expenses: $330 - $74.46
Profit: $255.54

Then I had my weekly business meeting with Addie and we tallied it all up. There were only two weeks left of summer. Our P&L looked like this: $330 in revenue and $74.46 in expenses, yielding a profit of $255.54.

We actually lost money on the Jessica account that first week. Yes, she had paid us $20, but from there we had to pay Amit $10. And we had to buy a second bucket and net, which cost $22.55. So while the new account had brought in $20 in revenue, it had also carried $32.55 of expenses. For that first week, we lost $12.55 on that client. But I was still optimistic because, once again, the second net and bucket were a one-time expense. The following week we'd take in $20 of revenue and only have $10 of expenses, a net gain of $10.

It was weird, because even though our top line was growing fast, the bottom line wasn't. I discovered something important about profit margin. That's what Dad said you call the difference between the price you charge and your costs. It's the money you get to keep. As our little business got more complex to be able to grow and handle more customers, the profit margin went down.

When I was just cleaning Dad's pool, my margin was 100%, which means I could keep 100% of everything I made. I had no costs. I was using Dad's bucket and net. Once I added Larry as a customer, I had to buy my own equipment and my profit margin came down because now I had real costs. But it was still a good margin.

Now that we had added Jessica as a customer and had to hire Amit, we had big costs and our margin was smaller. So we made less with each client. Which meant we needed more clients.

"Wait, so we actually lost money on Jessica, the new customer?" Addie was surprised.
"Yes, but don't worry, it's just this first week we're negative. Next week it's going to be positive because we don't have to buy a net and bucket each time, remember? And by the third week we'll have

recouped all our money and made a small profit."

"So it's an investment," Addie said.

"Hey, you're good! You're getting the hang of this."

Jessica Account

Week	Revenue	Costs	Profit / (Loss)
1	$20	$32.55	($12.55)
2	$20	$10	$10
3	$20	$10	$10
Total	$60	$52.55	$7.45

It turned out to be a good investment indeed because we got three more calls about our pool cleaning service. One from a man named Andre, one from an old man named Lee, and another from a woman named Luisa. Our new flyers were working.

It got to where Addie had to start keeping a schedule so we wouldn't accidentally double-book again. This is what our new schedule looked like.

Monday	Tuesday	Wednesday	Thursday	Friday
Elspeth	Larry	Andre	Lee	Dad
Luisa	Jessica			

It turned out Luisa needed her pool cleaned on Mondays, the same day we had Elspeth scheduled. So I sent Amit to clean her pool the following week. Since everything had gone so smoothly with Jessica, I fully expected there would be no problem.

I was wrong.

I was at Elspeth's, halfway through cleaning her pool, when she handed me her phone. I looked at her, puzzled.

"It's for you," she said. "Your mom's on the phone."
"My mom?"
Elspeth shrugged.

My mom had called to tell me that Luisa had called her twice wondering why no one had been to her house to clean her pool. I scribbled down her number.

"Mom, I've got to go." I hung up quickly and asked Elspeth if I could borrow her phone again.
"Of course."
I called Amit's mom. She told me Amit had left fifteen minutes ago.

Fifteen minutes ago! He was supposed to be there an hour ago.

I called Luisa and apologized profusely and explained Amit would be there very soon. She sounded a little annoyed but agreed to wait.

I thanked Elspeth profusely (it was that kind of day, a profusely kind of day) for lending me her phone and got back to work. I tried to finish as quickly as I could so I could rush over to Luisa's house to check on Amit.

"I'm sorry to rush out," I said. "But I've got a situation I've got to take care of."
"Take Milton with you."
"What?"

"You never know how these situations will go."

"It's not that kind of situation."

"Still, I'll feel better if Milton is with you. Just in case."

Milton barked. I could only assume he too thought it was a good idea.

"Are you sure?"

"Yes, he needs a walk anyway. You know how rambunctious he gets when he's cooped up."

"I sure do."

Milton barked again.

"Ok. I'll bring him right back."

"No rush," she said. "Hey, I heard about Francine. I'm sorry things didn't work out."

"Francine?" I had no idea what she was talking about.

"She's my neighbor. I told her about your pool cleaning service. She had gotten your flyer and asked me about it. When I called Addie to confirm our appointment today she told me Francine had decided against it."

I immediately felt my face flush and my ears turn red. *She knew!*

"Oh," I managed to mumble.

"Anyway, it's too bad it didn't work out. I told her you always do a good job."

I felt so embarrassed. "Yeah, I think I kind of messed that one up."

"Don't worry about it," Elspeth said kindly. "These things happen."

"I guess so."

Milton started bumping against the door and moaning. He was anxious to get going. So was I. But all I could think about was how everyone knew what I'd done, everyone knew about my phone call with Francine and how I'd messed it up. I felt my head getting hotter. I was sure my face was bright red at that point.

Milton started scratching at the door. And then I suddenly felt a huge wave of relief. I was so glad I told Addie the truth. She would've found out anyway. Elspeth would have told her. I had no idea Francine and Elspeth knew each other. I thought nobody would find out. I was so glad I didn't lie to her. I would have been found out. And this would have felt ten times worse. A hundred. No, a thousand times worse. Everyone would think I was a liar.

"I think you better get going," Elspeth said, bringing me back to reality. "I don't think Milton can stand another second cooped up in here."
"Yeah, me too," I said. "I don't think he wants be cornered here either," I added awkwardly. "I mean cooped. Not cornered. Cooped up. What you said, that's what I mean."
Elspeth put her hand on my shoulder gently. "See you next week?"
"Um, yeah, of course," I blurted out, thankful she wanted me back. "See you next week."
I don't know who bolted out the door faster, me or Milton.

I had to admit Milton was growing on me. The one time he wasn't home when I was cleaning Elspeth's pool, I missed him. Elspeth said he was at the groomer. I missed Milton jumping in the water and swimming while I swept up leaves. I'd tell him some clump of leaves looked like a T-Rex and he'd bark in agreement. He always agreed with me. I liked that about him.

Milton and I got to Luisa's house right as Amit was leaving.

"Hey what's going on?"
"What do you mean?" Amit looked suspiciously at Milton.
"I mean why are you showing up late to clean her pool?"
"Sorry, I was helping my brother fix his bike and it took longer than I thought."
"Amit! We told her you'd be there at 10."
"I know, and I tried."
"Amit, she was freaking out. She called my mom twice, wondering where you were."
"What's the big deal? I still cleaned her pool."
"The big deal is that we promised people we'd show up on time.

That's one of our selling points. And we need to keep our promises."
"Ok, sorry, I won't be late next time."

Amit said he was sorry, but the way he said it told me he didn't actually think he'd done anything wrong. I was so mad I could feel my ears were getting hot.

Seriously.

I didn't know what to do with Amit. Maybe hiring him had been a mistake. But if I fired him, could I find someone better? Would I really fire him? He was my best friend. I tried to think of what to tell him.

So what would *you* do?

Would you tell Amit he was fired?

Would you say nothing and hope it didn't happen again?

Is there something else you could do?

Chapter 14

The Boss Of Something

"I thought you said you weren't really going to be my boss," Amit said.

"I know." We were walking back slowly, so I would have enough time to think about what to say as we walked. Milton was panting softly as he followed alongside us.

"I guess I was wrong," I said at last. "This is my first time doing something like this, and I'm starting to realize business is different than friendship. There has to be a different set of rules."

"So you actually *are* going to be my boss?"

"Yes." It was hard for me to say. "If you want to keep cleaning pools with us, then I have to be your boss."

"Hmmmph." Amit grumbled. "I don't know about that. I'm not sure I want a boss telling me what to do."

We kept walking. I was worried. I tried to think about what worried me the most.

"That's ok," I said. "I'm not sure I'd want to have a boss either, if I were in your shoes."

Amit nodded but said nothing else as we kept walking.

"The important thing is that we're still friends," I said. "We'll always be friends."

Milton barked in approval

"How does that work?" Amit asked.

"Well it's up to you if you want to keep cleaning pools. If you don't, I'll figure something else out. No hard feelings," I assured him. "But if you do, then you have to agree to work by my rules. And you have to agree, that during the time you're working, I am your boss and you'll follow my rules.

"Whoa dude! That's intense."

"I know," I agreed. "But the more I think about it, that's the way it has to be. We have clients depending on us. The rules have to be different. It can't be like when you're coming over just for fun, and it's not a big deal if you're an hour late. I mean it's annoying, but ultimately it's not a big deal. But it *is* a big deal when we tell a client we'll be there at a certain time, and then we're not. They plan their day around our appointment."

"I guess I can see that."

"And a lot of times, they need their pool cleaned because they're going to have a swimming party. And if we don't follow through on our promises, we'll get fired. And we don't want that."

"Yeah, that's not good."

"So I need someone who will follow rules. I hope it's you, because you're my best friend, and I like working with you. But if you don't want to deal with rules, and you don't want me as your boss, then I understand. What's important is our friendship, and I know that if we can't agree on the rules, we'll end up fighting and that will hurt our friendship."

Milton barked again in agreement. Smart dog.

"So what are the rules?" Amit asked.

"I don't know. That's a good question. I need to think about it and write them down. Are you still interested?"

"Well it *is* nice making some extra money. And I don't mind the work, it's kind of fun, actually."

"Ok, why don't I think about the rules, write them down, and then we'll meet and see if we can agree."

"Ok, Mr. Boss."

"Hey, you're still the boss of penalties." I tried to lighten the mood. Amit laughed.

"It's true," I said. "You always beat me when we have penalty shootouts."

"It's good to be the boss of something." Amit smiled.

We said goodbye, and then I went to go drop Milton off. It was really cool, because Elspeth said I could take Milton with me on my pool cleaning jobs anytime I wanted.

"Really?" I tried not to smile too wide.

"Really," she said. "I would feel better knowing he's with you. Especially if it's a new client you've never met. Milton's got your back. Right Milton?"

Milton barked loudly.

"Are you sure you don't mind?"

"Not at all, it's good for him to get extra exercise. I wish I could walk him more myself, but I get so busy sometimes. Besides, I think Milton likes you."

Milton barked twice.

She gave me an extra leash she had and said I probably didn't need it, but just in case Milton got rowdy I should have it. I thanked her and said goodbye. When I got home, I told Addie it was time for a business meeting.

"Yes!" Addie got excited. "I love business meetings. Let me get my notebook," she said.

"Now that we have an employee we need to have rules."

"We have an employee? Who?"

"Amit."

"But he's your friend."

"I know, and that's the problem. He is my friend. But if he's going to clean pools for us, then he's also our employee during that time. And we need to have clear rules to know what to expect, so there's no more misunderstandings."

"That makes sense. So what are the rules?"

"Well, the first rule should be that you have to get to the appointment on time. In fact, the rule should be that you get there five minutes early."

"That's a good one." Addie wrote it down.

"And rule number two should be, that if you can't make it to an appointment, you have to let us know the day before so we can figure something out."

"I like that one. What else?"

"I'm not sure…Oh, I know. You have to take your net and bucket to each appointment. And you have to take care of our tools."

"That's important," Addie agreed. "They cost a lot of money."

"Yes they do."

"What else?"

"I'm thinking."

"Oh, oh, oh! I know!" Addie exclaimed.

"What?"

"Let's look at our flyer. Whatever we promise there should be a rule, so we make sure we keep our promises."

"That's a great idea. If we're going to promise our customer something, we need to make sure our employee knows about it so they can follow through."

Addie went and got her sketchbook and pulled out a drawing of our flyer. We both looked it over.

"We need to be friendly," I said.

"And polite," Addie added.

"That's good."

"What else?"

"I think that's it. We Probably don't want to make too many rules, or Amit won't want to work with us."

<u>The Rules a.k.a Standard Operating Procedures</u>
1) Arrive 5 minutes early to every appointment
2) Notify us the day before if you can't make it
3) Always bring your net and bucket
4) Take care of your equipment
5) Be polite and friendly

"We should have T-shirts," Addie said.

"T-shirts? That's so random."

"No, I don't think so. How will new clients know that it's us? If we send Amit or someone else to clean someone's pool, they're probably expecting Chance or Addie. Because that's what our flyer says."

"You're right. That's brilliant Addie."

This is why I had her as my partner. We always had better ideas when we brainstormed together.

"So we need a name for our company."

"What should it be?"

"Hmm, I don't know."

"What about The Dolphins?"

"The Dolphins? I think that just makes things more confusing."

"Octopus?"

"No, no, no! It needs to be more specific. What about...Kids Cleaning?"

"Eww, no," Addie said. "That sounds like we'll wash and scrub dirty children."

"C&A Company?"

"C&A?"

"Chance and Addison."

"We sound like lawyers."

"We don't want that."

"No, we definitely don't want to sound like lawyers."

"Let's think about it some more."

"Ok."

We agreed to keep thinking about it, and we each agreed to keep a notebook handy where we wrote down possible names as we thought of them. But none of them really stuck.

The next day I went to go clean Andre's pool. The visit was uneventful. In and out in an hour and a half, another twenty dollars earned, and another happy customer.

The following day I went to go see our other new client, the old man Lee. That visit was anything but uneventful. I picked up Milton on the way. The big dog started wagging his tail and barking when he saw me. I was happy to see him too.

I was glad I had Milton with me. The house we went to was the last one on the street. It seemed kind of run-down. Even though it was early in the morning, the whole house was kind of dark as I knocked on the door. I gave Milton a reassuring pat as we waited for the door to open. Whether it was to reassure him or me, I wasn't exactly sure. Milton started to emit a low level groan, as if to get his chest ready to bark strongly.

At last the door opened. An old man in a white undershirt opened the door. There was a coffee stain on it. He was walking with a cane.

"Who are you?"
"I'm here to clean your pool."
"My what?"
"Your pool."
"Oh! My pool."
"Yes."
"Good. $20 right?"
"Yes sir."
He seemed to think about it for a minute. "Come on in."

He led us to his backyard and the moment I saw his pool I was shocked. The water was green and slimy. Well that's were you could even see the water. Most of the surface was covered with piles of rotting leaves that were at least a half-foot tall. It had probably been years since that pool had been cleaned.

I gulped. I didn't know what to do. It would probably take all day to clean his pool. It didn't seem worth it for only $20. I turned to look at the old man, and he gave me a pitiful smile. I thought about leaving.

But on the other hand we did say we would clean your pool for $20. I was torn. I didn't know what to do.

So what would *you* do?

Would you clean his pool anyway?

Would you ask for more money?

Or would you walk away?

Chapter 15

Submariner

At first I was mad because I thought it was unfair. I thought the old man with the coffee-stained shirt was trying to take advantage of me and have me clean his very dirty pool for only twenty dollars. And that seemed very unfair.

But as I looked around inside the rest of his house – a broken chair, spider webs on his curtains, duct tape on the closet door – I began to realize, here was someone just struggling to keep everything clean and working.

He probably wasn't trying to take advantage of me, he just found someone who said they were willing to clean his pool for cheap. The mistake had been mine, not his. I learned an important lesson that day, one that would serve me well in the future. We hadn't asked any questions when people called us to clean their pool. We just assumed all jobs would be the same: a fairly easy two-hour pool cleaning, scooping up dead leaves and emptying drains. I realized then that we needed to ask more questions in the beginning to figure out if someone was going to be a good customer or not.

We were so excited to sign up new customers, it hadn't occurred to us that not all customers are good customers, and we needed to be careful picking who we agreed to work with, or we'd end up in situations like this. I decided I would talk to Addie after this, and we would come up with some good questions to ask anyone who called about our pool cleaning service.

The old man was very patient as he stood waiting for me to decide what to do. I decided to make the best of the situation. I didn't want to go back on my word. We had said we would clean his pool for $20. I could almost hear the voice of my dad in my head, reminding me that keeping my word is more important than having to put in a few extra hours of work.

So I decided to clean Old Man Lee's pool, even though it was a lot of work, and indeed it was. I must've sweated buckets worth of sweat. Have I mentioned how hot it was that summer? Then something happened. The more I cleaned, the more I started to feel like I was really helping him. There were some clients like Sir Larry, whose pool didn't actually get very dirty, where it felt more like he was helping *me* by giving me something to do to earn a little extra money. But this felt different. Old Man Lee most certainly needed help, and if I could make his life a little bit better by cleaning out his gunky, yucky pool then I was glad to do so.

He seemed genuinely happy as he watched me work. Slowly his backyard came to life as I removed bucket after bucket of debris from his pool. After a while he was smiling wide, and I think he got inspired because he started raking his little patch of grass and tidying up the area around the pool. That was its own reward, to see a little bit of joy return to this old man, and to feel like I made a difference. Some payments are even better than money. I hope I never forget that. Business should be about more than just making money. Ultimately it should be about making people's lives better.

Plus I got one other reward that day, a very special one I still have even now. It was towards the end of the day, and just as I expected, it was a very long day. There was one corner of the pool that still had a lot of leaves. I had methodically been working my way from one end of the pool to the other, corralling all the loose debris into that corner. When I dipped my net into that last holdout, I felt something move. I was so startled I almost dropped the net.

"Something's moving!"
"What is it?" Old Man Lee called out.

"I don't know, but it's definitely alive."

"Be careful!"

Milton started barking at the dead leaves.

"I think I see it!" I couldn't actually see it, but I could see movement under the dead leaves as it tried to evade my net.

"Did you get it?"

"Almost. I thought I had it, but then it swam under my net."

"Like a submarine."

"Yeah, he's a little submarine that keeps escaping."

I tried again, and again. On the third try I scooped it out of the water.

"A turtle!" Old Man Lee cried out.

It was indeed a turtle. And he was scared. He pulled his little head back into his shell, hoping we'd leave him alone and go away. I gently laid him down inside a big pot that had some dirt in it.

"What would you like to do with it, Mr. Lee? If you feed it, I'm sure it would make a good pet."

"Oh I don't have time for that, I can barely take care of myself."

"I bet he'd make a good companion."

"Why don't you keep it?"

"Because it doesn't belong to me, he was in your pool so he's yours."

"You can have him," Old Man Lee said.

"Sweet. Thank you, Mr. Lee."

"What will you call him?" he wondered out loud.

"Submariner."

"Submariner?"

"Yes, didn't you see the way he kept submerging himself to evade capture? He'd dive deep like a little submarine."

And that's how I got Submariner. I've kept him ever since. He's a good reminder of all I learned that day, and keeping perspective on what was important in business. Old Man Lee had been so grateful for the work I'd done, I almost felt bad taking his money. But I also knew I had worked hard to earn it. Both of those things felt good.

As I walked home from Old Man Lee's house, I happened to pass the street where I had first knocked on doors trying to find customers. I saw the curb where I'd sat down to eat some of the candy the nice old lady had given me. That felt like so long ago. That was even before I met Sir Larry and had my very first real customer. I decided to take a moment and enjoy what it all meant. I walked to the curb and sat in the same spot I had sat in several weeks before. I gently lowered the bucket to the pavement and checked on Submariner. I had put a tiny bit of water in there for him to swim around.

The summer was almost over, there was only one more week left. I couldn't believe everything that had happened since that first time Dad told me he'd give me ten bucks to clean the pool. I thought about all the times I had wanted to give up, all the challenges that I had faced. I was grateful for them, because each one of those problems had forced me to think of solutions and take risks that made the business better. They made *me* better.

I'm glad I didn't quit when I was tempted to call it a day and spend the summer eating ice cream and playing soccer. Those first weeks of summer when I was only making ten dollars sometimes felt like I was going nowhere. Even when I was making twenty and forty dollars a week with Dad and Larry still felt like I was floundering sometimes. I'd love to tell you I knew all along it would work out and that's what kept me going, but I'd be lying. I had no idea if I would make my goal. It was only at the very end of summer, with six customers, a partner and an employee that it all came together. But it only came together because I stuck with it all those weeks with just a handful of clients. That was an important thing to remember.

I got up, wiped the sweat off my forehead, picked up my net and bucket and started walking home. I turned around to look at the curb as I left and thought to myself, next time I'm here I'll be riding Midnight Blue.

Week	$ per Week	Customers
1-4	$10	Dad
5	$20	Dad
6-7	$40	Dad, Larry
8-9	$60	Dad, Larry, Elspeth
10	$80	Dad, Larry, Elspeth, Jessica
11	$140	Dad, Larry, Elspeth, Jessica Luisa, Andre, Old Man Lee

When I got home I put Submariner in my pocket and went to Addie's room.
"Good news sister!"
"What is it?"
"We have a new partner,"
"A what?" Addie looked steamed.
"A new business partner is joining us."
"Chance!" Now she was really boiling. "You can't just add another partner without checking with me first."
"But, Addie, you'll like this partner. He knows a lot about dirty pools."
"I don't care what he knows. It's not fair, Chance!"
"I promise, you'll like him." I could feel Submariner wiggling around in my pocket. "He doesn't say much. I seriously doubt he'll ever disagree with you in a business meeting."
Addie curled her fists just like she always did when she was mad.

I decided it was time to stop torturing her, so I pulled Submariner out of my pocket and handed him to her. She wouldn't take him.

"What's that?"

"Our new partner."

"What? A turtle?"

"His name is Submariner."

"Submariner?"

"That's right. I found him while I was cleaning a pool today. He was swimming around under all the leaves, like a submarine."

Addie looked skeptical.

"Go ahead, you can pet him." She gave me one more mean look, just so I knew she didn't like being messed with. Then she picked Submariner up out of my hands.

"He's cute."

"Not really, but he's mine now. Old Man Lee said I could keep him. And don't worry, he won't be disrupting any of our meetings. He's a silent partner."

"I thought you really did add a new partner."

"C'mon, Addie. I wouldn't do that to you."

"I don't know, you do have crazy ideas sometimes."

"Not that crazy. But there is something we need to talk about. Go get your notebook."

"Yay! I love business meetings." Addie handed Submariner back to me while she fetched her notebook. I set him down on the table.

"Ok, I'm ready."

"Not all customers are good customers," I said, mostly thinking out loud. "I never knew that till today. We need to figure out how to tell them apart."

"They're not all good?"

"No, they're not."

"Why not? I mean, a customer is what we need, right? What we keep trying so hard to get."

"Yes, but we need to try hard to get the right customer, not just any customer."

"How can a customer be bad? I don't get it."

"Well like today, Old Man Lee—"

"I thought you liked him."

"I do. That's not that I mean. Maybe good isn't the right word. I don't mean like he's not a good person. I mean he's not good for business. I pretty much spent the whole day cleaning his pool, which is definitely not worth twenty dollars."

"Twenty dollars and a turtle."

"True, but still. Not worth it. If every customer is like that, we won't survive. I'll be too tired to work the next day, Amit will quit, we won't have the time to take on new customers, we'll all get discouraged." Addie tapped her pencil against her notebook, startling Submariner who crawled back to me. "That's no good."

And then it hit me. "It's like leaves in the pool, right."

"Huh?"

"Well that's why people hire us, to scoop them out. To keep them from piling up. If we don't, the filters get all clogged up, the water gets all dirty and then you can't use the pool."

"Yeah, and?"

"Don't you see, this is the same thing!" I stood up, excited I could explain it. "If we let too many bad customers in, they'll clog us up and then we can't function. We need to filter them out, just like dead leaves."

Addie pointed to the screen on her windows. "Or mosquitoes."

"Exactly!" I patted Addie on the back. "We need to screen the bad customers."

"How do we do that?"

"By asking questions. We can't just agree right away to clean someone's pool. We need to figure out if it's going to be good situation, if it's going to be worth it."

"What should we ask?"

"That's what we're trying to figure out," I said, sitting back down. "That's what this meeting is about."

What do you think, are all customers the same, or are some better than others?

What questions would you ask, to screen customers?

Are there any customers you would say no to?

Chapter 16

Mr. Dubious

"Well the first one is pretty obvious, right?" Addie said. "We should ask how long it's been since they had their pool cleaned."
"Yep, yep."
Addie wrote that down.
"Maybe we should ask what color the water is," I said.
"Really?"
"No, but I wish we could. If their water is green, that's not a good sign."
Addie laughed. "What can we ask them then?"
"Let's ask them how often they clean their pool. It's almost the same as asking what color their water is."
Addie took more notes. Then she looked up. "I know another one!"
"What?"
"We could ask how big their pool is."
"That's great, Addie. Good thinking."
She smiled. "Anything else?"
"I think that's a good start."
"So what do I tell someone who calls and they haven't cleaned their pool in a long time, or their pool is really big. Do I tell them no?"
"Hmm...good question."
We both sat there thinking.
Finally, Addie said, "What do you think, Submariner?"
Submariner pulled his head back into his shell.
"I told you he wouldn't really take over our meetings."
"So do we just turn them down?" Addie asked again.
"Maybe we charge them double. I hate to turn down a customer, but we need it to be worth it."
"Then they'll just say no, like Francine."
"That's ok," I said, "one less leaf in our pool to clog us up."

"Got it." Addie finished taking notes.

New Customer - Screening Questions
1) When was the last time you had your pool cleaned?

2) How often do you clean your pool?

3) How big is your pool?

A couple days later Amit came over. It was a Saturday and we had nothing to do, no work, just fun.

"Hey Boss," he said as he hopped out of his mom's car and jaunted to the door. He liked calling me that, and I could never tell if he was just joking around and having fun with it all, or if he was being sarcastic and resented me slightly.

"Hey Amit." It was probably both. And that was ok. Amit had agreed to work by the rules I gave him, and so far he had done a good job with the two clients we had entrusted to him. He had earned the right to tease me.

As usual, we hung out in the backyard and kicked the ball around.

"Let's play lightning," I said.

"Cool! I'm goalie." The rules of lightning are very simple. One person is goalkeeper, the other is the striker taking a penalty shot. The striker kicks the ball and if he misses, the keeper throws it back to him and he kicks again, and again, until he scores. If he makes a goal, you switch: the goalie runs to the penalty spot to shoot and the striker runs to the goal to cover, he's now the goalie. The point is to do it all as fast as possible. First person to run to their new position usually wins.

We each grabbed one of Mom's flower pots to set the goal.

"Hey, not so wide," I told Amit.

"Why not?"

"Because it's more fun if the goal is narrower. Harder to score."

"That's just because you're not as good a goalie as I am."

"No seriously, it's better if it's harder to score."

"Ok, boss." This time there was no mistaking it. Amit wasn't joking around when he called me boss. He didn't like that I always told him what to do. That stopped me cold. It didn't use to be this way, before he started working for me. No one was really in charge, we kind of just took turns deciding. We'd argue sometimes, of course we'd argue, but it didn't seem like one of us would always win. I suddenly realized that now it did. I was so used to telling him what do to and getting my way when it came to cleaning pools, it had seeped over into all of our interactions.

I didn't want to lose my friend.

I needed to keep business and friendship separate. When we were working together, I was the boss and laid down the rules. But when we weren't working, well Amit was my best friend and I wanted to keep it that way. I couldn't be the boss when we were hanging out, just like he couldn't just be my friend when he was cleaning pools, he was my employee.

"Hey, no, you know what, you're right," I said, moving my pot back to where it originally was. "Let's go with the wider goal."

"You sure?"

"Yeah, definitely. You're right. I need to get better at goalkeeping. Wider is better."

"Sweet. Ok take your best shot."

I aimed it to the far left corner. Amit dived just in time and managed to just barely punch it out with his left hand. No goal.

"Dude! That was awesome!" I congratulated him.

"You wish you could do that," he said, and tossed the ball back to me.

"I do," I conceded. "You're the boss. The Boss of Keepers."

And then I took another shot. I kicked it as hard as I could.

The last week of summer flew by quickly. Old Man Lee didn't call again for another pool cleaning, but that wasn't too surprising. I don't think he could afford regular service like our other clients.

We actually got one other call that last week and got another customer. So our second batch of flyers had yielded 5 new customers: Jessica, Luisa, Andre, Old Man Lee, and the last customer, Max. It turned out the quality of the flyers had a big impact on the response rate. The better our flyers were, the more new customers we got. In the end our success rate was 5%, much better than the 1% we got the first time.

<u>Marketing Strategies – Success Rate</u>
Second Flyer (New Selling Points) – 5%
Knocking On Doors – 2%
First Flyer (Old Selling Points) – 1%

I was a little bit sad when summer ended. Starting this pool cleaning company had been so much fun and I had learned so much. It was time to go back to school. I was going to miss it. The weather would soon start to turn cold anyway. Pool season was over. Several clients, including Sir Larry and Elspeth, wondered if we would clean their pools next summer. That made me very happy.

Addie and I had one last business meeting to review our P&L. It was a little hard to add up the numbers because Submariner kept crawling over the ledger. We were sitting at the kitchen table taking turns holding the turtle in our lap. We would get so focused on the numbers, we'd lose track of the little green guy until there he was, crawling all over our profit and loss statement.

Our final tally looked really good. Those last two weeks when things were really happening and we had 6 regular customers (Dad, Larry, Elspeth, Jessica, Luisa, and Andre), plus two one-time customers (Old Man Lee and Max), we made $280. When you add it to the $330 we had earned up to that point, we ended the summer with $610 in revenue.

Profit & Loss Statement - FINAL

Revenue
Dad Pool Cleaning: $190

Larry Pool Cleaning: $140

Elspeth Pool Cleaning: $100

Jessica Pool Cleaning: $60

Luisa Pool Cleaning: $40

Andre Pool Cleaning: $40

Old Man Lee Pool Cleaning: $20

Max Pool Cleaning: $20

Total Revenue: $610

Expenses
Net & Bucket: $22.55 x 2 = $45.10

100 Photocopies: $9.68 x 2 = $19.36

Amit's Wages: $10.00 x 5 = $50.00

Total Expenses: $114.46

Profit/Loss
Revenue – Expenses: $610 - $114.46

Profit: $495.54

The last two weeks of summer we had to pay Amit for the two customers he serviced: Jessica and Luisa. We paid him $10 each time, so we had $40 in new expenses. Our total expenses for the summer were $114.46. Our profit was $495.54. Pretty good, if I do say so myself.

Subtracting the $50 I earned on my own left $445.54 to split with my partner. Divided by two meant I got $222.77. So my total earnings that summer were $272.77. Mission accomplished. I had enough to buy Midnight Blue. With tax, the bike cost $240.75. So I even had $32.02 leftover, enough to buy Submariner an aquarium at a secondhand store.

"What are you going to do with your half of the money?" I asked Addie.
"I'm going to buy a bicycle of course."
"Hey! How come you're always copying me?"
"Because you're my big brother."
I couldn't help but smile at that. "And your partner, don't forget."
"And my partner." Addie beamed.
"Do you know what the best part of having Midnight Blue is?"
"What?"
"Well with a bicycle we can expand our service area next summer. Right now we can only clean pools that are within walking distance of our house. But next summer we can go twice as far on bikes."

That night Dad had Mr. Dubois over for dinner. I call him Mr. Dubious, both because it was really hard to pronounce Dubois, and for reasons that will soon become apparent.

"Mr. Dubois is a venture capitalist," my dad introduced his guest to the rest of the table.
"What's a venture capitalist?" I asked over mouthfuls of spaghetti.

"It's someone who invests in new ventures, hoping to make a big return on their investment," Mr. Dubois said. I tried not to stare at that impossibly thin line in the middle of his brow that kept the two masses of hair apart.

"What's a venture?" Addie asked. "Do you mean an adventure?" Dad chuckled at that. "It sort of is, actually. A venture is a new business."

"We have a venture," Addie said.

"So I hear." Mr. Dubois chuckled. Dubiously, I might add.

"Yes! We clean pools," Addie said excitedly.

I had been waiting for this moment ever since Dad and I ran into him at the coffee shop. I cleared my throat. "And we now have seven customers."

"Seven," he repeated.

"Will you invest in us?"

"Kids having a venture? I've never heard of such a thing."

"We made a lot of money this summer," I pressed our case.

"Did you?"

"Yes $610."

"And a turtle!" Addie added.

"Wow." Mr. Dubois whistled. Dubiously, once again.

"So will you invest in us?" I asked.

"I'm sorry kids, but I only invest in real ventures." Mr. Dubious turned to my dad sheepishly.

"But we *are* a real venture," Addie insisted.

"That's it!" I shouted.

"What?" Everyone turned to look at me.

"What's it?" Addie repeated.

"I have it!"

"Have what?"

"Our name, Addie our name!"

"What is it?"

"We are KidVenture. That's the name of our company."

"Yes!" Addie agreed enthusiastically.

"We'll prove that kids can have real ventures, just like grownups."

117

"We sure can."

And that is how KidVenture got its name. And that's also when I vowed that one day we'd make Dr. Dubious regret not investing in us.

See, I promised I'd tell you the story. And now you know.

What do you think, can kids start and run ventures?

Are you ready to start yours?

What was the most important lesson you learned from Chance & Addie?

Acknowledgments

A huge thank-you to Raife Giovinazzo who carefully read a first draft and whose insights, suggestions and encouragement significantly improved the story. Big thanks also to Carey Wallace who reviewed a draft and offered critical feedback that helped me make the book better. I am very grateful to both for their friendship.

A very special thank-you to my four children –Sebastian, Dahlia, Zoe and Silas– who were my test readers through multiple drafts. As they asked questions, laughed, or frowned in confusion, I took notes and made edits. The book has more sparkles, bananas, turtles and groggy dogs thanks to them. I had so much fun reading to them, and even more, writing for them.

KidVenture started as a vague idea I bounced-off my wife and trusted partner, Elin. Her advice and loving support have been invaluable, in this venture as in all endeavors.

Made in the USA
Middletown, DE
10 December 2021

54570735R00076